"I WANT TO KNOW THE TRUTH, KATE," HE SAID, NOT stopping until he was in front of her, only the smallest space separating them. "And I want to know it now."

What else could she say? "I told you the truth," she said calmly. "You chose not to believe it." No matter what she said to Jack Ringo, what had happened to her was something he was never going to believe.

"Then make me believe you," he said. His gaze bore into hers, blue penetrating blue, delving past the tears in her eyes, past the hurt and anger he saw there . . . searching . . . probing.

Kate shook her head, trying to break the spell developing between them, realizing its dangers, its irresistible draw. "I can't. I . . ." Her shoulders sagged and she felt suddenly exhausted. "I don't know how."

His hands reached out for her, circled her waist, and drew her to him.

His mouth was hard and hot on hers, his kiss demanding, almost savage. Even through the haze of her own overwhelming passion, Kate felt that part of Jack that he kept hidden. It emanated toward her now, reached out and beckoned to her like a tangible force. And like a beam of moonlight drawn toward earth, with no ability to change paths or resist the pull, she was drawn to him.

WHAT ARE *LOVESWEPT* ROMANCES?

They are stories of true romance and touching emotion. We believe those two very important ingredients are constants in our highly sensual and very believable stories in the LOVE-SWEPT line. Our goal is to give you, the reader, stories of consistently high quality that may sometimes make you laugh, sometimes make you cry, but are always fresh and creative and contain many delightful surprises within their pages.

Most romance fans read an enormous number of books. Those they truly love, they keep. Others may be traded with friends and soon forgotten. We hope that each LOVESWEPT romance will be a treasure—a "keeper." We will always try to publish

LOVE STORIES YOU'LL NEVER FORGET
BY AUTHORS YOU'LL ALWAYS REMEMBER

The Editors

GUNSLINGER'S LADY

CHERYLN BIGGS

BANTAM BOOKS
NEW YORK · TORONTO · LONDON · SYDNEY · AUCKLAND

To my own Jack, with
love forever.

GUNSLINGER'S LADY

A Bantam Book / September 1997

ISBN 0-553-44591-X

Published simultaneously in the United States and Canada

Bantam Books *are published by Bantam Books, a division of Bantam Dou-*
bleday Dell Publishing Group, Inc. Its trademark, consisting of the words
"Bantam Books" and the portrayal of a rooster, is Registered in U.S.
Patent and Trademark Office and in other countries. Marca Registrada.
Bantam Books, 1540 Broadway, New York, New York 10036.

PRINTED IN THE UNITED STATES OF AMERICA

OPM   10 9 8 7 6 5 4 3 2 1

PROLOGUE

Tombstone, Arizona
August 1881

"This is not happening," Kate Holliday said.

"Guess again, lady," the bespectacled whiskey salesman sitting on the stagecoach seat across from her replied.

The wildly careening coach bounced over a rut in the road and momentarily left the ground.

Kate pressed her feet to the floorboards and fought to stay on her seat.

The savage screams of a half-dozen Indians split the air and sent a chill down her back. Something smacked hard against the rear of the coach. Kate whirled, grabbed the window ledge with both hands, and poked her head through the glassless square. An arrow whizzed past her nose. She immediately dived back into the coach.

Grabbing the bowler hat that sat on his head, Henry Simmons hit the floor.

This isn't happening, Kate told herself. This couldn't be happening. The Apaches were supposed to be on the reservation, not the warpath.

Another arrow shot through the window and pierced the seat salesman Simmons had just vacated. Another instantly followed, slamming into the door frame.

Kate screamed and yanked her hand from the window ledge.

"Hang on, folks," the driver shouted down.

A war lance plunged into the side of the coach. The driver's whip snapped the air, and the bloodthirsty cries of their pursuers seemed to become even louder, drowning out every other sound.

Kate closed her eyes, fighting the terror that was threatening to engulf her. "Everything's going to be all right," she mumbled. "Everything's going to be all right." She'd been in worse situations.

The coach swerved around a curve in the road.

A nerve-shattering shriek sliced through the din of noise surrounding her. Kate jerked around and caught sight of an Indian pony racing alongside the coach, its rider's face and chest smeared with black and red paint.

Fear, bone-deep and intense, turned her blood cold. Everything wasn't going to be all right. This was it . . . she was going to die.

The Indian's cold, merciless black gaze met hers. Another shriek ripped from his throat, and his tomahawk sliced through the air toward her.

Kate dived for the floor and collided with the whiskey salesman.

The tomahawk slammed into the coach's door, nearly splitting it in half.

Kate stared at the sharp edge of the ax protruding through the wood, only an inch from her bent knee. She frantically fumbled through her petticoats, pushing them aside to get to the small derringer Doc had given her years earlier and which she always kept strapped to her thigh.

Henry Simmons threw his arms around her. "We're gonna die. We're gonna die," he screamed.

Something crashed against the coach and caused it to jerk violently.

"Let go," Kate yelled, and pushed Simmons away with a jab of her elbow.

A screech nearly shattered her eardrums. She was grabbed from behind and her head yanked back viciously. Kate looked up into black eyes that were as cold as night.

"No," Kate snapped. She slammed the heel of her hand into his chin as hard as she could.

Startled, he lost his hold on her.

Kate scrambled across Simmons and the seat.

The Indian's eyes flashed excitedly at the challenge she'd provided. He yanked the tomahawk from the door, sending the splintered wood flying, and, releasing his hold on the doorjamb, bounded into the coach, squatting with one foot on each seat, the whiskey salesman rolled into a ball and quivering beneath him, Kate sitting on the seat and staring at him defiantly.

With a murderous grin on his face, he grabbed for her.

Kate jerked the derringer free of her garter belt and fired. The bullet's impact threw her assailant against the window ledge. A wail split from his lips, and he jumped back up. Lunging at Kate, he encircled her throat with one hand while with the other he grabbed a knife from a sheath at his waist.

Kate twisted in an effort to escape, gasping for breath.

The Indian brought the knife slashing toward her breast.

Kate fired the derringer again.

A strangled cry broke from the Indian's lips. He jerked upward, arched back, and fell.

"Get him off, get him off," Simmons yelled as he thrashed frantically about beneath the Indian's body.

The coach bounced furiously. Suddenly everything tilted.

Henry Simmons screamed and clung to the doorjamb.

Kate flew from her seat and into the wall.

The coach plunged down a small cliff, rolling onto its side.

Kate felt herself smash against the door, and finally she tumbled out.

ONE

Tombstone, Arizona
August 1997

"Jack Ringo, you're being archaic."

He stopped in the doorway and turned around. "What?" Annoyance edged his reply.

"You heard me," his sister said. "Archaic, old-fashioned. That's you."

He glared at Liz, who smiled sweetly at him from her seat on his eldest daughter's bed. But he wasn't fooled, and as far as his little sister was concerned, he never had been. The smile might be sweet, but there were defiance and challenge in her eyes. Always had been, always would be. She loved to goad him, and he loved to see her frustration when he ignored her. Jack's gaze darted to his daughter Tiffany, standing stiff-shouldered near her dresser, every inch of her face covered with makeup and her usually long, straight blonde hair piled atop her head in a mound of curls.

If Cathy had been alive, she'd have known how to handle the situation. "I don't care what Aunt Liz says," he growled softly to Tiffany, while pointedly ignoring his sister. "You're eleven, Tiff, you're *my* daughter, and you're not wearing makeup to—"

"Oh, Jack, really," Liz said. "What's the big deal? It's only for a costume."

"Children, children, please, you're upsetting my new little plants with all this bickering." Marion Ringo slipped past her son and into her granddaughter's room. "I swear you're going to make my darling devil's ivy go into shock, just like you did to my fig-leaf." She looked at Jack. "Anyway, Jacky dear, Jessi needs you in the kitchen."

"Don't call me Jacky."

She waved a hand at him. "Oh, fiddle. You've been Jacky since the day you were born. Now go on with yourself. Jessi's in a tither."

"Great," Jack muttered. If it wasn't one female driving him nuts, it was another. He turned and walked down the hall. The previous day he'd taken them all up to Tucson for a day of shopping and doing whatever they'd wanted. He'd planned this as a quiet day, his last until after the festival. Instead, from just about the moment he'd opened his eyes that morning, his family had done their best to turn it into the Ringo Family Circus and Unforgettable Day from Hell.

"Daddy, Daddy, Miss Kitty won't take care of her babies," Jessi wailed the minute he stepped into the kitchen. "They're gonna die."

He glanced at the basket full of kittens, then at the

calico cat who had strolled across the room and sat in the center of a patch of sunlight flowing in through the window. As if giving birth was the easiest thing in the world, and something she'd already forgotten she had just done, times six, Miss Kitty ignored Jessi's wailing and began to preen.

Jack walked over to where his nine-year-old sat in the corner, the basket of newborn kittens in front of her. At least Miss Kitty had cleaned them before she'd deserted. "Well," he said, hunkering down, "if she doesn't come back in a few minutes and start making like a mom, I guess we'll have to take care of them ourselves, won't we, Jess?"

She turned to look at him, all wide blue eyes and pert nose beneath a mass of chestnut curls. "Really, Dad? We can do that?"

He touched a finger to her nose. "Yeah, Jess, we can do that. Grandma will show you how. She helped me with a bunch of puppies when I was a kid and their mom died."

"Wow." Jessi turned her attention back to the six kittens wiggling about in the basket. "Can we put them in my room tonight for my sleepover?"

Jack frowned. "What sleepover?"

"Grandma said you wouldn't mind."

Jack felt like groaning. It wasn't enough that he lived with five females, but they were always inviting in more. And his mother was always telling them he wouldn't mind. It was going to be another of those times on the Ringo ranch when he felt like General

Custer at the Little Big Horn—totally surrounded and outnumbered.

"Squawk. Grandma loves Jacky. Grandma loves Jacky. Squawk squawk."

"Shut up, Parsons," Jack snapped, glaring over his shoulder at the huge parrot who sat on his perch near the window.

"Shut up, Parsons, squawk, squawk. Shut up, Parsons."

"Great," Jack muttered, wondering if anyone but KaraLynn would really mind if Parsons suddenly disappeared.

As if thoughts of his six-year-old were a silent summons for her to appear, she suddenly rolled through the kitchen doorway, across the room, crashed into Jack's back, and fell on her rear end.

KaraLynn smiled up at him as Jack twisted around to look down at her. "Hi, Daddy."

He frowned, though he felt like laughing. It was almost impossible for him to be mad at any of them, which wasn't good for discipline, so he did his best to fake it whenever needed. "KaraLynn, how many times have I told you not to wear your in-line skates in the house?"

"But Grandma said it was okay."

Grandma said it was okay. That was the story of his life. The influence of a grandmother who was more than a bit eccentric, and an aunt who was more than a bit defiant and a little too liberated for Jack's tastes, was not always healthy. But he had no choice. After Cathy had died, he'd come to rely on them, and so had the girls.

KaraLynn looked past Jack. "Ooh, kitties." She scrambled onto her hands and knees for a better look. "Can I have one, Daddy? Huh? Please? Huh? Can I?"

"You have Parsons."

KaraLynn's face screwed into a pout. "But I want a kitty too."

Jack sighed. "We'll see." Which he knew meant he was already doomed. Someday he'd have to figure out how to look into the eyes of a six-year-old and say no. He stood and walked toward the doorway. "I'll get Grandma."

"Ssshoooo!"

Jack stopped and turned back. "Somebody have a cold?"

"Thimbles," Jessi said, pointing toward the table.

Jack looked in the direction Jessi indicated, and his mouth dropped open as he stared at the tiny poodle, who, snuggled up against Boozer, the giant bloodhound Jack had adopted two years earlier, stared back at him from beneath the kitchen table. "What the . . . ?"

"Isn't he neat?" Jessi asked. "Auntie Liz told Tiff that Squirrel-faced Alice had a purple dog when she lived in Tombstone, so Tiff dyed Thimbles for the festival and said she's going as Alice."

The dog sneezed again.

Jack decided not to voice the fact that Squirrel-faced Alice had been a prostitute. He was not about to let his daughter attend Tombstone's annual Old West

Festival as a prostitute. He walked across the room and bent down in front of the dogs for a closer look. Boozer didn't even stir, but continued to snore. Thimbles looked up at him with huge, tear-filled brown eyes that were almost lost within a mass of bushy purple hair. "If I don't miss my guess," he said, "Thimbles is allergic to the dye Tiff used on him."

"Daddy, I want a kitty," KaraLynn said again.

"Kitty, squawk. Kitty, squawk."

Thimbles sneezed.

Jessi giggled.

A woman screamed.

TWO

A soft moan slipped from Kate's lips as awareness crept back into her mind. Her skin felt hot, her lips dry, and her whole body ached. She tried moving her arms and felt nothing but pain, along with the sensation of a thousand needles being stuck into her flesh. Would she still hurt if she was dead? Opening her eyes, she expected to see herself surrounded by golden-winged angels or, maybe more realistically, by a half dozen of the devil's little pitchfork-wielding minions. She turned her head slightly, and her vision focused just as the tip of her nose scraped against the needle of a prickly pear cactus.

The plant hovered half next to her, half over her like a sprawling green monster. Kate raised her head, just a touch, and glanced toward her feet. The large plant hugged the entire right side of her body, and judging from what she was feeling, a good part of it was also hugging her underside.

She cursed softly. First Indians, then the stagecoach crash, and now a giant cactus. What was next? Snakes? Trying not to move her body, she looked around for the stagecoach. It was nowhere in sight, which meant she'd probably been thrown out and it had kept on tumbling. But to where? It couldn't have gone that far. The land all around was mostly flat.

"Probably behind me," Kate mumbled on a sigh. She'd escaped the Indians only to land in a cactus patch surrounded by a picket fence.

Picket fence? She raised her head again but couldn't see anything else. Why would a picket fence be around cactus out in the middle of nowhere—unless there was someone nearby who'd built it? "Help." The word came out as little more than a croaked rasp. No one answered, and Kate suddenly realized she shouldn't have made a sound. What if that bunch of bloodthirsty savages heard her?

Before the thought had time to instill her with fear, a shadow swept over her. A scream caught in her throat as she looked up and saw a man standing over her. The sun at his back left her with a vision of nothing more than a tall, menacing silhouette. She cringed, certain that at any moment, when he bent down to slice off her scalp, the last thing she'd see was the same grotesquely painted red-and-black face and cold black eyes she'd stared into when he'd tried to plunge his knife into her breast.

He reached a hand toward her. "Can I help you?" The rich, deep voice startled her.

He moved to stand beside her, and Kate found herself staring into a pair of midnight-blue eyes that she'd always considered the most beautiful she had ever seen on a man. A wave of relief swept through her, so profound, it brought tears to her eyes. "Ringo?"

Surprised, Jack frowned and the helping hand fell back to his side. He didn't recognize her, didn't know her, yet she knew his name. His gaze swept over her. He'd never in his life forgotten a beautiful woman, and he definitely found this woman beautiful, even if half of her was hidden from his view within the voluminous folds of an antique gown.

Forgetting for a moment that he was more than mildly annoyed at her sudden intrusion into a day that had already begun a rapid descent into chaos, his gaze moved over her swiftly and assessingly.

Kate returned his stare and lay perfectly still, realizing that if she didn't move, she didn't hurt. The bright rays of the sun softly caressed his broad shoulders and danced off the ragged strands of chestnut hair that covered his head and kissed the back of his neck. She'd never been so glad to see anyone as she was to see Ringo standing there. Another movement caught her eye and Kate noticed the huge dog who sat down next to him. He had the saddest face she'd ever seen on an animal, and she felt a need to comfort him. Instead, she forced herself to ignore the pain that came with moving her arm and raised a hand to Ringo, noticing as she did that the palm of her fragile black lace glove was torn beyond repair. "Help me up, would you, Ringo?"

Her words instantly cut through the fantasy that had begun forming in his mind and brought it to an abrupt halt. A shudder of shock went through Jack at realizing what he'd been doing. He shrugged the last of the ridiculous thoughts aside and looked at her hand but made no move to take it.

Kate shifted slightly. Cactus needles poked into her backside, her shoulder, and her arm, and it felt as if she were lying on a rock the size of a horse. There was no way she could get up on her own without making the situation worse, and his hesitation was doing nothing to soothe her temper. "Johnny, dammit, help me!"

She remembered too late the one thing Johnny Ringo didn't like was to be told what to do.

Johnny? The name set him back.

Kate nearly groaned in despair. His frown deepened and a shadow invaded his eyes, turning them darker, unreadable. It was a look she'd seen on his face many times. Assessing, calculating, and teetering on the edge of either icy coldness or searing heat. It was a look that could chill a man's blood, or turn a woman's to flame, depending on what had brought it on. But right now she didn't have time or patience for his games or his touchiness. She was about to snap at him again when she let her gaze move quickly over his features, wondering suddenly if she'd been mistaken and he wasn't Johnny Ringo. The thought unsettled her. Ignoring her discomfort, her scrutiny turned assessing and minute. He had the same brown hair as always, a mass of raggedly cut red-gold-touched waves, one rebellious curl falling forward whenever he removed his hat, the same rigidly cut cheekbones, sharp jawline, straight nose, and deeply hollowed cheeks. The intense, magnetic blue eyes were the same she remembered, too, as were the sharply defined lips that always seemed drawn up slightly on one side, in either a sneer of antagonism or a devilish, challenging smile. Kate's gaze dropped to broad shoulders and bare arms that were sinewy golden lengths of muscle. Made to hold a woman close, she'd always thought secretly whenever she'd looked at him.

Then she noticed his clothes, pants cut off above the knee and a shirt that had no sleeves or collar and was so thin, she could almost see through it to the curly dark hairs she'd often wished she could run her fingers through.

Her gaze dropped to his hips. Kate felt another flash of unease, this time tinged with more than a little fear. Johnny would never be caught anywhere without his guns. She glanced at the hands that hung at his sides. Gunman's hands. Agile, long-fingered, and as quick as lightning. Just like Doc's.

She looked back up at his face, at those cool, fathomless blue eyes. She didn't understand why he was wearing such unusual clothes, why he was without his guns, or why he was acting so strangely, but she knew it was him, because no other man had eyes like Johnny Ringo's.

And no other man held a grudge the way he did, she thought, exasperated and figuring he'd been hovering over her, taunting her, for at least two or three minutes. With her whole body hurting like the dickens from being tossed around in the stagecoach, then stuck with a hundred cactus needles, she felt like screaming at him, but she knew that would only rile him and make matters worse. He'd probably turn around, walk off, and leave her there just for spite.

Kate forced her voice to remain calm when she spoke again. "Johnny, I know you're still angry with me because of Doc, but I'm not with him anymore. We haven't been together for some time. Not that way." She tried to smile through her pain. "I guess I shouldn't have flirted with you in front of him the way I did, though."

"Land sakes, Jacky, what are you doing just standing there?" Marion said, approaching. "Help the poor woman out of that mess."

Kate saw an older woman move up beside Ringo and nearly gasped at the woman's attire—a top that was little more than a camisole and pants that, like Ringo's, left almost her entire legs bare. Huge silver-and-turquoise earrings hung from her ears, at least eight of her ten fingers were adorned with rings, and a dozen silver bracelets jangled at her wrists. Kate couldn't believe what she was seeing.

"Hey, Dad, what's going on?"

Jack glanced up at his eldest daughter. What *was* going on? That's what he wanted to know. But he didn't mean it quite the same way Tiffany did.

Kate looked at the young girl approaching them. She couldn't be more than ten or eleven, had on an outfit even scantier and more improper than the older woman's, as well as more paint on her face than any whore Kate had ever met.

Kate glanced at Ringo. *Dad?*

"She a friend of yours or something, Gram?" Tiffany asked the older woman.

Jack threw his hands up, momentarily forgetting about the woman in his cactus patch. "Tiffany, go in the house and take off that makeup."

Kate moved slightly, too engrossed in what was going on around Ringo now to worry about her own situation. Makeup? Scandalous clothes, no stagecoach in sight, Johnny Ringo with no guns and being called Dad. Something was definitely very wrong, but she'd be hornswoggled if she knew what it was.

A needle suddenly jabbed into the soft flesh of her side and she shrieked.

The older woman whirled toward Ringo. "I swear, Jacky, if you don't help that poor little thing out of there right this minute, I'm going to push you into that cactus patch you love so much and you can get a few needles stuck in your backside too."

"Geez, what happened?"

Another woman suddenly appeared within Kate's view. She was tall, shapely, not much younger than Kate, and bore a striking resemblance to both Ringo and the older woman. At her side was another child, this one about eight or nine, with long, curly hair almost the exact shade of Ringo's, big blue eyes, and little ruby earrings in each ear. Kate groaned silently. If she was going to attract an audience, it would be nice if at least one of them would help her up. And why were they calling Ringo *Jacky* and *Dad*?

"I'll help her, Mom," Ringo said, as if reading Kate's mind. "You take the girls inside." He reached out, grabbed Kate's hand, and jerked upward, hauling her quickly to her feet.

"Oh, be careful, Jacky," Marion said. "Poor thing." But now she was looking at the cactus, not Kate.

Kate winced as several dozen cactus needles tugged at her skin, some breaking off, some falling out, others digging in.

Marion shook her head. "Oh dear, I think I heard it cry when all its little needles were pulled out. You should be more careful, Jacky."

Jack ignored his mother and the "girls" who hadn't moved, and glared at Kate. "Who are you, and what the hell are you doing in my garden?" His tone was rough, brusque, and held not one hint of compassion over the fact that half of her body probably looked like a porcupine and definitely felt like a pincushion.

"Taking a nap," Kate snapped, wincing as she lowered her arm. The movement caused a needle to gouge deeper into her back, which nudged her temper a notch higher. "What did you think I was doing?"

"Mercy, mercy," the older woman crooned, dancing past Ringo to stand between him and Kate. She looked up at Kate and touched a hand lightly to her arm. Her bracelets jangled merrily while her rings caught the sun, the reflection nearly blinding Kate. "Don't mind my son, honey"—she threw Jack a glower that would wither most men—"he can be truly rude sometimes. Downright grumpy. Just like the movie, except he's not an old man." She chuckled softly and shook her head. "He's already killed several of my plants with his temper tantrums."

Kate looked at the woman warily. Killed her plants with tantrums?

"Now, sweetie, I'm Marion Ringo, Jacky's mother, and I want you to come on into the house with me and the girls"—she glanced at the others and motioned them toward the house—"so we can get those nasty cactus needles out of you, and put a little disinfectant on you, just in case."

Kate hoped the woman's disinfectant was Kentucky bourbon and not that rotgut whiskey most of the saloons in town served, because she could use a good shot too. She looked around for the coach again, but it was nowhere in sight. Nor were any Indians, the stagecoach driver, or that whiny little whiskey salesman. Kate frowned. Had she walked away from it? Perhaps staggered through the desert, delirious, then passed out here? It was a possibility, but wouldn't she remember *something*? She looked at the older woman as they started to walk toward the house. "We were attacked by Indians."

Marion nodded. "I thought it was something like that. Probably those darned Hansen boys again. I swear, someday they're going to really hurt someone with their games and carryings-on.

"Hansen boys?" Kate echoed.

Marion nodded again. "Live down the road a couple of miles. But they don't come around here much anymore. Not since they scared Jenny." Marion chuckled. "That's my pig. I got 'em good for that one."

"Grandma shot them with her slingshot," the youngest girl said.

Kate frowned. Ringo's tantrums had killed her plants and some boys named Hansen had attacked the woman's pig and she'd gotten rid of them with a slingshot?

"Indians," Marion snapped. "I oughta call their mother, that's what I ought to do. Dressing up and scaring people like that."

Kate glanced at the older woman out of the corner of her eye. Was she trying to say that the stage had been attacked by people dressed up as Indians? If so, she was wrong.

A blast of sound suddenly blared from one of the open windows of the house.

Kate jumped and turned toward it.

Marion chuckled at the look on her face. "That's Tiffany's room." She nodded toward the open window. "Jacky hates her taste in music, but I think it's kind of groovy. And our little plants just love it. Don't you, sweetie?" she called to a tall saguaro. "I think that's Meat Loaf singing." She glanced over her shoulder. "Lizzie, is that Meat Loaf?"

Meat Loaf and music? Kate glanced between the two women, quickly becoming convinced somebody was crazy, and it wasn't her. Unless she was imagining all this.

She looked at the house they were approaching and found it to be one of the strangest designs she'd ever seen. One story, with long wings jutting out from each side of the front door. The entire thing was painted beige, with bright turquoise trim on the windows and some kind of orange-brown bumpy things on the roof.

In front of what looked like a barn door at one end of the house was a bright red metal contraption sitting on fat, black wheels with silver centers.

They were halfway across the yard when a little girl—at least Kate thought it was a little girl—whirled out onto the porch. A mass of pale red curls stuck out from beneath some kind of multicolored pot she had on her head, her knees were bandaged with huge blue pads, and she had black boots on her feet with bright pink wheels attached. She stopped by grabbing on to a pillar. "Gram, what's going on?" she yelled, and looked at Kate. "Wow, who's that?"

"KaraLynn," Jack snarled, "I told you to take those skates off and stop using them in the house." He glared at the child.

"Okay, Daddy."

Daddy? Kate's mouth almost dropped open in shock. She looked from the older woman to the young woman to Ringo to the children. This was an insane asylum. It had to be. A giggle of hysteria filled her throat, and she fought it down. She didn't know why Ringo was there, why he was letting these children call him Daddy and the older woman act as if she was his mother, but it had to be because they were all touched in the head. Ringo was from back east. He'd told her once he had no family left, and even if he'd lied and still had a mother, playing Daddy was just something she could never fathom Johnny Ringo doing. At least not the Johnny Ringo she knew.

She stared at him again. Could he be Ringo's twin brother? Kate rejected the idea almost the moment she thought of it, and her gaze swept over all of them again. Somehow she'd been thrown from the coach, landed in the garden of an insane asylum, and the inmates had come out to greet her.

She was in trouble.

Jack watched his "girls" usher the stranger into the house and shook his head. It wasn't as if he didn't have enough trouble with them already, now they were taking a looney tune under their wing. A beautiful looney tune, but a looney tune all the same. The woman had to be crazy, there was no doubt about it. Anyone who would run around the countryside in bone-cracking, dry, one-hundred-degree heat dressed in an old-fashioned long gown, gloves, petticoats, pantaloons, and high-top lace shoes the day *before* the Old West Festival was scheduled to begin, then manage to fall into a cactus garden that was completely surrounded by flat land and a picket fence, had to be crazy. Certifiably crazy. Either that, or she'd staged the whole thing because she wanted something from him.

A frown tugged at his forehead. But what could she want? He glanced toward the road in the distance. There were no cars in sight, no one with a camera, nothing. But she'd known his name. Tombstone wasn't near as big as it had been in its heyday, so everyone who lived in the vicinity now knew everyone else. There were a lot of strangers in town for the festival, he reasoned—but they didn't know his name, he argued back. She had, though she'd called him Johnny instead of Jack, and he wouldn't be Johnny until to-morrow, when the festival started and he dressed him-self up as his great-great-great-grandfather.

"Come on, Boozer," he said, and trudged toward the house, fully aware that the way his luck had been running that day, the worst was yet to come.

The huge brown-and-black dog lumbered after him faithfully.

Jessi assaulted him before he made it halfway across the living room. "Dad, can we have my slumber party in the sunroom tonight so we can watch TV? Huh? Please? Huh? And bring the kittens in too? Please." She blew a wayward strand of hair from her face.

"Yeah, fine," Jack grumbled, and made for the kitchen. At the huge plank table in the center of the room, Marion Ringo gently pulled cactus needles from their guest's back while Liz and Tiffany sat nearby and looked on, both wincing each time their guest did.

He'd already had his bad experience for the year with a woman, and he hadn't totally extricated himself from that situation. He certainly didn't need to become involved with another woman in any way, shape, or form. Jack walked around the table and stopped in front of Kate, who was staring at the stove with a puzzled look on her face. "Who are you?" he demanded. "And how in blazes did you manage to fall into my cactus garden when it's surrounded by flat land and a picket fence?"

"Jacky, you're being rude," his mother said, dab-bing antiseptic on Kate's arm. "Tsk, tsk."

He gawked at her. "And her throwing herself into my cactus garden and ruining it isn't rude?"

Kate forgot about the strange house, the strange room, and all the strange things in it as her temper flared and she fought to control it. If Ringo wanted to pretend he didn't know her, fine. She hadn't the faintest idea what was going on, or why he was parading around in such ridiculous clothes and masquerading as touched in the head, and she didn't care. All she wanted to do was get out of this place and back to town.

"Jacky. Shame!" Marion said.

He ignored her rebuke and looked back at Kate. "Well?"

Marion patted Kate's shoulder. "Ignore him," she said. Waving her hands in the air, bracelets jangling, she turned away. "Would you like some tea, honey?"

Kate was about to say no, wanting nothing more than to leave, then remembered she had a long walk back to town and a cup of tea would go a long way in sustaining her. "Thank you, tea would be nice." She glared at Ringo.

"Who are you?" he demanded again.

Kate took a deep breath, intent on being polite for the sake of the older woman and the children, even if Ringo wasn't. "Ringo, you know very well I'm Kate Holliday."

"You're who?" Jack snapped.

"Oh, this is getting good," Liz said to Tiffany.

"I swear," Kate said, before Jack could go on, "I just don't understand what happened. I was on the stage to Tucson when it was attacked by Apaches and forced off the road. The coach crashed, and I don't really know how I got—"

"*What?*"

Kate jerked back at his one-word blast.

"Kate Holliday? Stagecoach? Apaches?"

His eyes suddenly reminded her of a thunderstorm: dark, unpredictable, and ominous. Silver slivers of color, like hot and angry bolts of lightning, sliced through the infinite blueness. A scoffing laugh split from his lips. "The festival doesn't start until tomorrow, lady, and I've already had a helluva morning, so quit the games and just give us the truth, okay?"

"Games?" All of Kate's good intentions to hang on to her temper immediately evaporated. Jumping from the table, she jammed clenched fists onto her hips and, eyes narrowed, glowered back at him. "You're a fine one to call me a liar, Johnny Ringo, since lying is about all you ever do, whenever you're not brawling in a saloon or drawing down on someone, that is."

"Brawling in a . . . drawing down . . . ?" Jack looked at her incredulously, taken aback by her accusation. "Are you totally nuts, lady, or what?"

"Nuts? What's that mean?"

"You know damned well what it means. Out to lunch. Missing a few bolts." Her puzzled expression fed his frustration, to say nothing of his temper. "Crazy," he nearly thundered. "Insane. Touched."

Kate stiffened. "No, I am not touched, Ringo, I'm Kate Holliday."

"Yeah, right, and I'm Wyatt Earp."

Her eyes narrowed. "Since when does Johnny Ringo pretend he's Wyatt Earp?"

"Look lady, I'm not—" Jack stopped as a thought flashed through his mind. She'd obviously been in town and seen one of the wanted posters of his great-great-great-grandfather. Or saw a picture in a history book. Jack looked exactly like him, so she was probably assuming he'd be masquerading as his outlaw ancestor during the festival. Well, she was right, though why she was insisting on this playacting a day early he had no idea. Maybe she was trying to win some radio contest or something, but her act was beginning to get on his nerves big time, and he hadn't been in a real good mood to start with.

"Look, call me Johnny Ringo tomorrow, *Kate,*" he said, with sarcastic emphasis on her name, "and I'll answer you. Might even draw down on you, but not today, okay? Now"—he forced a smile to his lips—"what's your real name?"

He saw something hot and burning flash through her eyes.

"I told you, Ringo, my name is Kate Holliday, and you know it."

Jack threw up his arms in exasperation. "Okay, fine, wonderful. You're Big-nosed Kate Holliday. Doc's cheating, conniving woman."

Kate's mouth dropped open as rage and indignation swept through her like lava from an active volcano.

THREE

"How dare you!" she snapped, her tone as hot as fire, her eyes blazing with indignation. Suddenly the others in the room failed to exist. "I've never cheated on Doc, and the name Big-nosed was merely a practical joke of his that got out of hand." She thrust her face toward him, pointing to her pert, short, turned-up nose. "As you can see." Kate flipped the long, dark hair that had fallen free of its neat chignon during the coach crash over her shoulder and clenched her hands into fists in order to control the shaking her fury had brought on.

Once she had fantasized about making love to this man. Now all she wanted to do was ram her knuckles into his nose.

"Well, you keep preten—"

"And anyway," she said, practically throwing herself into his face, "none of what I do is the business of a lying, bloodthirsty, two-bit Cowboy who can't do anything better than swagger about, bully people, and follow Curly Bill Brocious around and do his bidding and killing for him."

"Whoa, boy," Liz whispered.

Tiffany and Jessi giggled, each poking the other in the ribs while staring at their father.

"Jacky," his mother said, stifling her own grin, "I'm ashamed of you. I think you owe our guest an apology. If Kate says she's Kate Holliday, then she's Kate Holliday."

"Yeah, Jack," Liz said, smiling, "you're being archaic again."

"What's arkic, Auntie Liz?" KaraLynn piped up while in the midst of rolling into the kitchen. Unable to stop, she rolled past everyone and bounced off the refrigerator.

For just about the first time in his life, Jack ignored his mother, sister, and daughters. He stared at Kate, total disbelief of what was happening keeping him speechless. The woman was either the best damned actress he'd ever seen, or totally insane, and with the wild look in her eyes and the way she was ranting as if it were the 1880s instead of the 1990s, he was pretty close to settling on the insane theory.

"Daddy, Kate could go to the parade with us tomorrow," Tiffany said, breaking the silence that had suddenly descended on the room. " 'Cause Aunt Liz is going as Josie Earp, and . . ."

Kate stared at the young girl. Josie *Earp*? Since when was Josie Marcus an Earp?

Tiffany continued, catching Kate's attention again. "I'm going as Squirrel-faced Alice and . . ."

Jack struggled to hold on to his temper. Were the Ringo women actually *trying* to drive him crazy today? "You are not going as—"

"I think I'd like some cookies with my tea," Marion chirped. She smiled. "Kate, would you like some cookies, dear?"

Kate nodded.

"Good." Marion grabbed a pack of cookies from a cupboard, then took two mugs from another and turned on a faucet.

Startled, Kate shrieked at the funnel of water that poured forth without anyone pumping for it.

Jack whirled on her. "I don't know who you are or what your game is, lady, but—"

Kate saw Marion shut the two cups of water in a white box, push a button on it, and the thing began to hum.

"—if you want to parade around town as the mistress who lived with a cold-blooded murderer," Jack continued, his words jerking Kate's attention back to him, "that is definitely your business. And if my mother wants to take you under her wing like another of her strays and pretend you're someone who died a hundred-some-odd years ago, fine, but stop filling my daughters' heads with this ridiculous fantasy act of yours." He spun around to face his daughters and mother, as if waiting for them to argue.

"Ah, c'mon, Jack," Liz said, "you're being—"

He whirled to glare at his sister, the anger in his eyes effectively silencing her. How, why, this stranger who'd invaded his home had the ability to plunge him into a fury with hardly saying a word confused the hell out of him, but he didn't feel like analyzing the situation at the moment, just controlling it. He tried to ignore the erotic little thoughts that kept popping into his head . . . like the fact that she was beautiful . . . that he wondered what her lips would taste like if he kissed her . . . that desire had suddenly nudged him in a way he couldn't ignore and was reminding him that he was a man who hadn't made love to a woman in longer than he cared to remember.

"And as for you," he growled at Liz, his temper worsened by the traitorous thoughts he was finding himself unable to control, "we are Ringos, in case you've forgotten, and as such I don't really think it's quite kosher for you to be parading around as an Earp during the Old West Festival. Do you?"

Liz stared defiantly at Jack, who stared defiantly back.

Kate looked from one to the other. What in the world did *kosher* mean? And what festival was he talking about? A steady stream of questions danced through her head, and more were added with each minute that passed. Unfortunately, the questions outnumbered the answers, which totaled zero at the moment.

Kate almost scoffed aloud. She didn't need answers, she needed to escape. But where were the nurses, the guards, who took care of these people? And why, she thought again, for the umpteenth time, was Ringo going along with all of this? She had heard him weave a lot of lies, seen the cold, icy glare that came into his eyes whenever a man made him angry enough to draw down. She'd seen him crazy drunk, crazy mad, and once she'd even seen him crazy passionate. That night Doc had interrupted them, and Johnny had been caught off guard and almost ended up dead. But Johnny had never actually sounded or acted really crazy in the head until now.

She glanced toward the doorway that led through the weirdly furnished parlor she'd seen on the way in. It also led to the front door. Would they try to stop her from leaving?

"Tea's ready," Marion said.

Kate turned and stared at Marion as she jerked a little bag from one of the cups and tossed it into the sink. She held the cup out to Kate, its dark liquid steaming.

"Here you go, dear. Do you want sugar? Or milk?"

Kate frowned. She hadn't boiled the water. She'd put it in the cup and put the cup in a white box that hummed. So how did the water get hot? And what was that little bag she'd pulled out of it? Kate took the cup, set it on the table, and began to inch her way toward the door.

One of the girls turned and looked at her.

Kate froze and smiled. If she could just get out of this place, she could make a run for it and head for town—if she could figure out which direction town was . . . and if she could stay out of sight of the Apaches who'd attacked the stagecoach.

That thought sent a chill snaking its way up her spine and almost brought a groan from her throat. She looked down at the little girl beside her, the one

Johnny had called Tiffany. Strange name. "Tiffany," she said softly, not wanting to draw Ringo's attention from the woman he'd called Liz. "Do the Indians bother you much out here?"

Tiffany frowned, then shrugged. "They come into town every once in a while," she said. "And Mrs. Two Horse owns a shop by the Birdcage."

Kate stared at the child. An Indian owned a shop near a birdcage? Kate felt her heart constrict as compassion swelled within her. How could such a beautiful little thing be so horribly touched in the head?

Unless it ran in the family. The thought came to her unbidden, and Kate felt a sense of horror rush over her as she looked back at Ringo. She'd heard of things like that. Was this what was wrong? Was this Ringo's family? Could this be why he'd always claimed not to have any? Because they were all crazy?

Not caring anymore who saw her, and determined no one was going to stop her, Kate whirled around and hurried toward the door.

"Oh, Kate," Marion Ringo called after her.

She paused, feeling caught.

"Don't be insulted by Jacky's rudeness and all this bickering. He's just had a bad day." She threw a nasty glare over her shoulder at Jack and hurried after Kate. "He had to bury Sheila Shefflera for me this morning. She was so big I couldn't do it by myself. I hated to see her pass away," Marion said as Kate stared at her, "but it was my own fault, leaving her in the sun like that. Her leaves just nearly burned to a crisp." She grabbed Kate's hand. "Please stay awhile and visit, or at least let

Jacky drive you into town. It's much too far to walk, especially in this heat and with that costume of yours. And I just couldn't bear another passing today."

Jack fought to keep his mouth from dropping open. It was bad enough his mother was rambling about one of her dead plants, but he couldn't believe she had just invited a total stranger, or some super-clever con, to have dinner with them.

"Thank you," Kate said, refusing to look at Jack, "really, but I have to go." She pulled her hand gently but forcibly away from the older woman, who was clearly out of her mind. "And I'd rather walk. . . ." She'd been about to add that it couldn't be that far to town, since she hadn't been on the stage for more than about fifteen or twenty minutes before it was attacked, but a quick glance at Ringo caused her to think better of saying anything about the stage again.

"Oh, but you can't walk," Marion said. "You'll get heatstroke, just like my poor Sheila did. No, I won't hear of it. Jacky will drive you." She glanced at him again, as if daring him to object. "And he'll behave. I mean, if you want to be Kate Holliday"—she smiled widely and clapped her hands, bracelets jangling noisily—"then you're Kate Holliday. And why not?" She looked at Jack. "Kate Holliday. Johnny Ringo." Her gaze darted to Tiffany and Liz. "Squirrel-faced Alice and Josie Earp." Her eyes widened in delight. "Maybe I should go as Diamond-toothed Heddie."

Jack nearly groaned aloud, convinced his mother had finally gone all the way off the deep end.

Liz laughed but didn't look all that pleased that her

mother was trying to talk the stranger into staying around. The girls began to giggle.

Jack heard them all in the background, but ignored them.

"Who?" Kate asked, curious in spite of herself.

Jack tore his astonished gaze from his mother and looked at Kate. She was beautiful, there was no denying that. Her long brown hair looked more like threads of silk, her face could have graced the cover of a fashion magazine, and for all he knew, maybe it had. Her nose wasn't big at all, in fact it was more . . . pert. Upturned, sassy, and pert. And her lips were full and made for kissing. At the moment he would have sold his soul to the devil to taste them.

Jack started. Sell his soul? What the hell was the matter with him? She was a space cadet bar none. A wacko or a con. Either way she was trouble. But he couldn't deny that from the moment he'd first looked down on her in the cactus garden, fleeting images of her lying in his bed, naked, passionate, and wanton as all hell, kept prancing through his mind.

He almost choked on the thought and forced himself not to tug at the inseam of his pants, which were starting to feel uncomfortably snug. Jack almost snorted. *Snug* was the understatement of the century.

Other than his "girls," as he called his mom, sister, and daughters, there hadn't been too many women in his life since his wife had died in an auto accident while on her way home from Tucson one night five years earlier. LeeAnn had been the only one, and he'd tried to correct that mistake almost immediately. The problem was, LeeAnn didn't want it corrected. And she'd never made him come anywhere near feeling as hot as he'd been in the last few minutes. Some men might have found that an enjoyable experience. Jack did not, especially since Miss Kate Holliday was obviously an escapee of Fantasy Island, a spaced-out addict, or an actress in town for a promo stunt who had decided, for some reason unknown to him, to try out her act on the Ringos. Though he knew there was no way his home could have been wired for *Candid Camera* or some home-video contest, he looked around uneasily, but spotted no little round lenses staring back at him.

"Jacky," Marion said impatiently, dangling his keys before him.

He glanced at his mother, then at Kate, and gave up the theory that she was a spaced-out addict. Her eyes were clear, and he'd seen enough druggies while in the army to detect the symptoms. With no cameras around, why would an actress bother with this charade? And aside from her attire and her insistence that she was Kate Holliday, she didn't really act crazy. Though what a crazy person really acted like, he had no idea. Unless he included his mother in that category. Usually he only thought of her as daffy or eccentric. "I could call you a cab," he said finally, his tone cool.

"Jacky!" his mother snapped in total disapproval.

"A cab," Kate repeated. She frowned, not having the faintest idea what a cab was. Her gaze moved over Ringo slowly as she again appreciated his good looks and tried to discern what he was doing in this place. Something had happened to him, that much was obvious. Maybe Curly Bill had done something to him. Maybe someone had hit him on the head with their gun butt and it had stirred his brain. Whatever had happened, she was no longer certain he was pretending with these people.

Kate felt a moment's regret. Though she would always have a soft spot in her heart for Doc, their love affair had been over for a long time. Before either of them had admitted their love was gone, however, she'd flirted with Ringo, whom she had always found devastatingly handsome—a fact that seemed enhanced by the sinister darkness that emanated from him and the sharp, sometimes biting sense of humor that had caught more than one person off guard, with fatal results.

Doc hadn't been amused, and whether he'd been genuinely jealous or merely made a show of it because of his ego, she didn't know. Doc had confronted Ringo one night while both were in Wyatt's Oriental Saloon. The two men had made a show of gunplay, whirling their weapons, drawing, and shooting bottles, and though Ringo had a reputation for being the fastest gun west of the Mississippi, Doc had beat him that night, and beat him bad.

Ringo had hated Doc before that. Afterward he'd loathed him. But he'd blamed Kate for the humiliation he'd suffered.

Her gaze moved appreciatively from his wide shoulders to his lean gunman's hands, down the long, sinewy length of his legs, and then back up to his face. Had he given up his guns? Or had they been taken from him when he'd come to this place? The question intrigued her. Then frightened her. She didn't want to be responsible for his death, and he'd definitely die if, crazy or not, someone came gunning for him and he didn't have his guns. The best thing she could do for herself, and maybe even for him, was to get out of there.

"Thank you," she said finally, "but I'll walk." She turned toward the door, making sure not to get too close to the huge, white metal box that sat near the doorway. Like the one on the counter the older woman had taken the tea from, this one hummed. Just as she was about to pass it, the smallest child rolled up to the box and shoved a glass against a lever set into its face. The thing hummed louder, and water came pouring from it into the girl's glass.

Kate nearly jumped a foot, then stared in shock.

"Oh, all right," Jack said, drawing Kate's attention again as his mother slapped his arm and whispered hurriedly. "It's five miles to town and one hundred and one degrees outside. My mother's right, you'll have heatstroke before you get anywhere near Tombstone." Unless you have a limo waiting on the other side of the hill, he thought wryly.

Kate assumed they were trying to tell her she'd swoon from the heat, which she knew was right. She'd been about ready to melt while riding on the stagecoach. "Thanks," she said, deciding she didn't want to be on a buckboard with a crazy person, even if it was Johnny Ringo. "But I'll be fine."

Guilt assaulted Jack. She was willing to risk heatstroke rather than ride in a car with him. Indignation clogged his throat like bile. Well, if she didn't like what he'd said to her, it was her own fault. She was the one who'd insisted on playing out a ridiculous charade.

Which is no excuse for rudeness, his better side countered.

Or lascivious thoughts, his conscience added.

Indignation turned almost instantly to intense suspicion. "I was planning on going into town anyway," he lied, "so it's no problem to give you a lift."

Give her a lift? He meant to carry her into town? The thought sent a shiver of excitement up her spine, which she immediately ignored. Kate smiled sweetly. "Thank you, no."

Turning before he could argue further, she hurried from the house.

The sweltering heat hit her full force the moment she stepped onto the shaded porch. Kate staggered under its onslaught, suddenly remembering how cool the interior of the asylum had been, and wondering how they did that.

She walked to the cactus garden, paused, and looked down at it, then at the surrounding countryside. Nothing but dirt and more cactus met her gaze. Why wasn't the stagecoach, or what remained of it, anywhere in sight? How could she have possibly been thrown so clear that she couldn't even see it now? And where was that repulsive, cowardly little whiskey salesman, Henry something or other? And the stage driver?

She cautiously climbed a small plateau and looked around, holding a hand up to shade her eyes from the sun's glare. She assumed the mountains on the distant horizon were the same ones she'd been looking at just before the stage was attacked. That would mean, she hoped, that Tombstone was to her right. After a few minutes of walking she came to what looked like a road but was covered in smooth, hard black rock. And there was a white line painted down the center of it, broken every three feet or so. She hesitantly put a foot onto its surface and pressed down, ready to jump away if her foot sank.

It didn't.

She pushed down harder. Sighing in relief, Kate stepped onto the pavement. Things would certainly have been a lot easier if Ringo wasn't touched in the head. Or pretending to be. She took another step. Her heart was beating faster than a horse could run, and her hands were clammy, but nothing untoward happened. She took several steps. Then several more. Finally, relieved, she began to walk. Maybe they'd covered the road with some newfangled stuff from back east, though she couldn't understand how she hadn't heard about it or noticed it while riding the stage.

It was several minutes before she realized she wasn't alone. Kate looked down at the huge dog who'd lumbered up beside her. She knelt down and, smiling, framed his face with her hands. "You can't go with me, you sad ol' thing," she said softly. She patted his head and stood. "Now go home."

He looked up at her soulfully.

Kate steeled herself against his heart-wrenching gaze. "Go home," she ordered again, more harshly than before. She waved her hands at him when he stood. "Go on, shoo."

Boozer turned and lumbered back toward the house.

Kate resumed her trek toward town. Minutes later a soft roaring sound seemed to surround her. Kate stopped. The sound grew louder. She stiffened. It sounded like the gates of hell had just opened and released its fury. With her heart in her throat, she spun around, intent on facing whatever new threat was coming her way and fully expecting to see a horse and rider bearing down on her, the rider's face covered with black-and-red paint.

Jessi turned from the table and looked at her grandmother. "Gram, where's my necklace?"

Marion put down the apple she was peeling and turned to open a cupboard. "I don't know, dear, where did you leave it?"

"Right here on the table," Jessi said, pointing.

Marion glanced at the table, then at Jessi, and shook her head. "Well, sweetie, obviously you didn't leave it there."

"I did too," Jessi insisted. "I took it off 'cause Miss Kitty kept batting at it when I was trying to pet her babies, and I put it right here on the table." Jessi's voice quavered. "And now it's gone."

FOUR

Its eyes glared at her, whitish-silver orbs bearing down on her relentlessly. Kate cringed, unable to take her gaze off the wide mouth, its lips drawn back in an ugly grin to reveal huge silver teeth. Above its sloping, pink forehead, a crown of crystal glittered wildly in reflection of the sun.

Kate thought of running, of screaming for Ringo, throwing herself to the side of the road, hiding behind a mound of sagebrush or some tumbleweed. But before she could do anything, the monster roared past at a dizzying speed, totally ignoring her and nearly sweeping her from the road with the force of wind it left in its wake. She stared after it, amazed, frightened, shocked. There had been people inside the monster. She'd seen them. A man and woman.

My God, was it devouring them? Kate shook her head. A delusion. It had to have been a delusion. Caused, no doubt, by all the peculiarities she'd endured at the asylum. Her mind was strained. She glanced down the road and saw the pink monster moving farther away from her. Kate squeezed her eyes closed. "I'm not crazy," she mumbled to herself. "I'm not crazy." When she opened her eyes again, the thing was gone, and she breathed a sigh of relief.

Then she remembered that one of those things had been sitting in front of the asylum. A red one. She glanced back warily. Maybe it had been sleeping . . . or was dead. That thought made her feel better.

Kate had been walking about five minutes when that same soft roaring sound penetrated her thoughts. Tension swept over her like a wave, drawing her shoulders stiff, turning her blood cold. This time she sprinted from the road without hesitation.

This one was blue.

She braced herself as it approached.

It sped past, totally ignoring her.

She breathed a sigh of relief. Then tensed at catching sight of a white one approaching. But it sped past too. She stuck a finger beneath the décolletage of her gown and pulled the fabric away from her skin. A trickle of perspiration slid between her breasts. She should have asked that Marion woman for a parasol. And a fan. And, she lifted her long hair away from her neck, a few hairpins.

Kate slipped out of the bolero-style jacket that matched her gown, noticing that one puffed sleeve was ripped partially from its seam. Taking a deep breath and releasing it slowly, she tossed the jacket down, trudged back to the road, and resumed her walk toward town. A half hour later she finally saw the roofs of several buildings come into view on the horizon.

"Thank heavens," Kate mumbled, feeling about ready to drop. The hem of her gown had collected more dust and grime than a gold digger probably got on his clothes in a week, her hair was damp with perspiration, and she felt as if her stockings and camisole were stuck to her like paste.

But she was alive, almost to town, and grateful that she never wore a corset.

The closer she got to the edge of town, however, the more uneasy she began to feel. She hadn't passed a rider, a stagecoach, a buggy, or even another person on foot since leaving the asylum. And several buildings she remembered the stagecoach having passed on their way out of town weren't where she recalled them to be. Kate frowned. The feeling that something was terribly wrong assailed her again.

Rounding a curve in the road, she stopped dead and glanced up at a building that sat on what looked like half a knoll, its front slope having been cut off for the road that passed before it.

MOTEL. The sign above the building seemed to stare back at her. What in blazes was a motel? And why did the building look so square and plain?

Kate cautiously turned away, took a step, and stopped, this time swallowing hard and wondering if she really wanted to continue. Across the street, opposite from the motel, sat a small, squat building. It looked like ol' Jeb Baker's shack, except that there were all kinds of those ugly monster things sitting in front of it, looking as if they were about to pounce. A sign over the door of the house said SOUVENIRS.

Kate inched her way toward the building, keeping a wary eye on the monsters in case they suddenly roared to life and turned on her. Lord, they all were so big and ugly, and each was a different color and shape. On the other side of the cabin Kate saw Boot Hill, but the cemetery looked different somehow. Then she noticed the sign.

BURIED HERE ARE THE REMAINS OF TOM MCLOWERY, FRANK MCLOWERY, AND BILLY CLANTON—KILLED IN THE EARP–CLANTON BATTLE, OCTOBER 26, 1881.

Kate's mouth dropped open. October 26. But it had only been August 15 when she'd left town. She couldn't have been gone that long. She'd remember. She'd know.

Forcing her legs to move, she walked toward the door of the cabin without turning her back on the resting monsters. She pushed the door open and backed hurriedly inside.

A bell above the door jangled, startling her, and a child somewhere in the room laughed. Kate spun around, expecting to see Jeb. Her hopes were dashed immediately.

Doodads of every type imaginable were everywhere: on tables, shelves, covering the floor, even hanging from the ceiling. Pictures of Wyatt, Virgil, Morgan Earp, and Doc were everywhere too. Indian baskets, blankets, and jewelry adorned the walls, while mugs and glasses emblazoned with the word *Tombstone* were stacked in front of the windows. Kate fought to keep her surprise and dismay from turning into panic.

"Hi, honey, you just get into town?"

Kate turned toward the woman who had spoken. She stood behind a counter, its surface littered with badges, wallets, and other trinkets. She had on something that looked like a sleeveless long john, its front covered by a likeness of Wyatt's face. Kate stared at the face on the woman's chest, then whirled about, snatched the door open, and ran back to the road.

A bright red monster roared up beside her and stopped.

Kate shrieked, ready to give in to her panic, and jumped back, heart racing, hands trembling.

Jack leaned out of a hole in the monster's side. "You okay?"

She stared at him, shocked, confused, and frightened. Ringo was inside the thing. It had eaten him. Kate felt a swell of despair.

"Kate?" Jack frowned. She looked half-frightened to death and even more bedraggled than she had when he'd found her in his cactus garden.

"Jacky, help her get in the car," Marion said.

Kate looked past Jack to his mother.

Suddenly the side of the thing opened toward her, and Jack stepped out. "Come on, get in. We'll take you to wherever you want to go."

Kate backed away. Her entire body began to tremble. She desperately wanted to close her eyes, order herself to wake from this nightmare, and find everything was back to normal. But she was too scared to close her eyes. Too afraid of what might happen if she did. "No," she whispered, and shook her head. "No, not in there." Turning, she stumbled, regained her footing, grabbed up her skirts, and ran.

"Kate?" Jack called after her.

She ignored him. Run, her mind said. She had to find Doc. He'd know what was happening. He'd help her.

St. Paul's Episcopal Church was the first building she recognized. So many things had changed, so many things were missing. And she didn't know why. She ran up Third Street, turned on Fremont, and paused. Fly's Photography Shop, Bauer's Butcher Shop, the O.K. Corral, the Papago Store, and the courthouse were where they should be. But where were the stagecoach stables? And a sign on the Bachelor House said TRADING CO. AND MUSEUM. She saw Schiefflin Hall, and ran up Fourth. The CanCan Restaurant was gone, and a sign on the building said TOURS, while across the street, where the Occidental Hotel should have been, was something called Book Trader.

Kate looked about frantically. People were everywhere, milling about and walking down the boardwalk, but they were all dressed like the people at the asylum. There wasn't a properly attired person anywhere in sight. Her eyes darted about. She'd known almost everyone in Tombstone, by face, if not by name, but she didn't recognize anyone now. She looked from one building to another, searching for something, anything, familiar. Where the Palace Hotel should have been, a sign said BIG-NOSED KATE'S SALOON.

"Oh no. No, no, no." She ran to the corner. The *Tombstone Epitaph*. The sign on the newspaper office gave her a moment's relief from hysteria. Her gaze moved slowly, warily onward. The Crystal Palace Saloon. Vogan's Alley Bar. Nellie Cashman's.

"Thank heavens." Kate sighed. "I'm not crazy."

She must have spent more time in the desert than she'd realized. Maybe she had been unconscious or delirious. Maybe she'd wandered for days without knowing it. But whatever had happened to Tombstone in that time, at least it had not all changed.

"Doc will know what's going on," she murmured to herself. She turned toward the Oriental, directly across from the Crystal Palace. Doc and Wyatt would be in there, and they would tell her what had happened. Gathering her long skirts, Kate dashed into the street.

A blaring noise rent the air, followed immediately by a spine-tingling squeal.

Before she had time to scream, jump, or even turn toward the noise, Kate felt something catch her skirt and yank it back. The force jerked her off-balance and threw her to the ground.

"Dammit, lady, you trying to get me killed, or what?" a deep, gnarly voice exploded nearby.

For the second time that day Kate found herself flat on her back, staring up at the sky. Confusion took a backseat to temper. She cursed softly and pushed herself upright.

Someone rushed forward to help her up. "Are you okay, lady?"

Kate stared, dumbfounded, not at the man who'd

accused her of trying to get him killed, but at the silver-and-black thing he was picking up from the ground. Still cursing, he swung a leg over it, then jumped slightly and pushed down on a lever with his foot. The thing roared loudly.

Kate shrieked and tried to scramble away, expecting the thing to pounce on her any second.

The man sat down on it as if it were a horse. It growled steadily and glared at her. "You going to move or what?" The man sneered.

Kate's gaze darted up to meet eyes covered by small, round mirrors.

This wasn't Tombstone. The thought sent a shudder of fear coursing through her. Not *her* Tombstone.

"Kate, Kate, are you all right?" Marion Ringo pushed through the crowd, shoving one very large, very heavy man aside as he hovered over Kate. "Move," she snipped at him.

Glowering at the five-foot dynamo who'd nearly knocked him off his feet, the man mumbled an obscenity and walked away.

"Kate," Marion said, dropping to her knees and clutching Kate's arms. "Are you all right, dear? Oh, mercy." She looked around, caught the gaze of the man on the motorcycle, and bouncing back to her feet, wagged her finger at him. "We never have auto accidents here. Never." She suddenly looked down at the carnation pinned to the front of her blouse. Her features screwed into an expression of distress. "Oh, and look what you've made me do to my pretty flower. It's crushed." She primped about its petals. "Poor little thing, are you all right?"

"She walked out in front of me," the man said with a snarl.

As if suddenly remembering Kate on the ground, Marion glanced back at her. "Oh, Kate, are you hurt, dear?"

Kate stared at the growling silver monster.

"Kate?"

Kate shook herself and, turning warily, looked at Marion. "Oh, ah, I'm fine, but . . . what is that?" She pointed at the motorcycle.

"A nasty man on a nasty little toy," Marion remarked.

Jack stepped up behind his mother and saw Kate. "Oh, great, her again," he grumbled under his breath. He instantly told himself that he didn't really care if she was all right or not, and just as instantly knew he was lying to himself. He looked at the man on the motorcycle. "What happened?"

"She ran in front of me, man, that's what happened. Stupid broad."

Jack glared at him, then turned back to Kate. He scrutinized her quickly. She seemed shaken but otherwise unhurt, and she was staring at the motorcycle as if she expected it to attack her. "I'll take her down to the first-aid station," he said to his mother.

Marion looked up at him, fire in her dark blue eyes. "You most certainly will not!" She took Kate's arm and steered her through the crowd and toward the boardwalk. "I was a registered nurse. We'll take her to the saloon and take care of her ourselves."

Jack followed. How had he known she was going to say that?

Behind him, the man revved his motorcycle.

Kate cringed and glanced over her shoulder at the sound as Marion steered her through a doorway and toward a table.

"Sit here, Katie," she said softly, then turned to Jack. "Jacky, I'm going to get a cloth to wipe the dirt off her gown. You get her something to drink."

Jack headed for the bar, knowing there was no use arguing with his mother. The sooner he got "Kate Holliday" her drink, the sooner Marion would see that she was okay, and let her go on her way.

Kate tried to relax. She looked around, regathering her wits. A long bar occupied one side of the room. Several poker tables were set here and there. And a wheel of fortune stood against the back wall. She jumped to her feet. She had to get to the Oriental. To Doc and Wyatt.

Jack saw her jump up and realized she was ready to bolt. Without thought of why he even cared, he dropped the soda he'd just retrieved from behind the bar and crashed past several chairs to intercept her at the door.

Kate crashed into him and took a staggering step back, feeling as if she'd just run into a brick wall.

"Where are you going?"

She stared up at him, temper flaring. "It's none of your—"

"Business?" Jack mocked. "It is as long as my mother keeps running to your rescue, and you keep letting her."

Kate stiffened in defiance. "I didn't let her. And I didn't need rescuing."

"Oh, really?" Jack mused. "You're here, aren't you?"

Kate drew herself up. "Well, it won't happen anymore. Now, if you'll please move."

If he let her leave, there would be no living with his mother. He knew that from experience and didn't feel like going through it again. "Answer my question first," he said, deciding to try to stall her. "Where are you going?"

"I told you, it's none of your—"

"I know, business. We've already covered that." He smiled. "So humor me. Tell me anyway."

She wished she had a two-by-four to split his hair with. Or her reticule. She glanced at her wrist. The reticule had obviously been lost in the stage crash. But if she'd had it, she could have swung it jauntily and smacked him alongside the head with the rock she always kept hidden in it.

"To the Oriental," she snapped finally, realizing he probably wasn't going to let her pass until she answered him.

"You're *in* the Oriental," he drawled.

Kate shook her head as if she hadn't heard him and tried to brush past him.

He blocked her with an outstretched arm.

Her temper flared. "Dammit, Ringo, stop fiddlin'

around and get out of my way. I have to get to the Oriental and talk to Doc."

His mood blackened at her mention of Doc Holliday. What was with this woman and her games? "I told you," he said sharply, "you're *in* the Oriental."

Kate stopped trying to figure out how to get past him and looked up into his eyes. They weren't laughing at her, as she'd expected, weren't twinkling with amusement at her expense. Something told her he wasn't lying. She turned and looked back at the room again, at the bar, the mirror behind it, the tables. Recognition swept over her. He was telling her the truth. Things were changed somewhat, but she was in the Oriental. Confusion settled over her. But where was everyone? She looked toward the poker table Wyatt always sat at when he was dealing cards, which was more times than not. He wasn't there. Her gaze jumped to where the faro table should be. It wasn't there, and neither was Luke Short, who'd always run the table. Frank Leslie wasn't tending bar. And Tinker wasn't at the piano. But if they weren't there . . . she turned back to the door, anxiety like a storm building within her breast. Something was wrong. She had to find them.

He saw the fear in her eyes and wondered at it.

"Come on, Katie," Marion said, walking up behind her and taking her arm.

Kate jumped, too deep within her own thoughts and fear to hear Marion's approach.

"Come in the back with me for a while and we'll

talk while you have your soda and I stitch up that little tear in your skirt."

"Gram, why don't we invite Kate to come home with us for dinner?" Jessi said, tripping along behind Marion.

Marion smiled. "Why, sweetcakes, that's a wonderful idea."

Jack almost groaned. He knew what was coming next.

"In fact," Marion said, clapping her hands and turning to Kate, "why don't you just come on home with us and spend the night, Katie?"

"Because she probably already has a room at one of the B-and-Bs in town," Jack said before Kate could answer. He looked at her expectantly, hoping she'd confirm his comment . . . and half hoping she wouldn't.

Marion looked at her too.

Kate frowned. "B-and-B?" she echoed.

"See, the poor thing doesn't have a room," Marion said. She stepped up beside Jack and lowered her voice to a whisper. "I think poor Katie was mugged, Jacky. She doesn't have a purse or anything, and she seems awfully confused."

"Which is exactly why she shouldn't be going home with us," he nearly growled. "We should call the sheriff. She probably belongs in the hospital." The mental hospital, he added silently.

At the mention of the sheriff, Kate spun around and ran toward the door. She should have known that whatever was going on, Sheriff Behan, who hated Doc and Wyatt, was behind it.

"Kate," Marion called after her.

Home. She'd go home, to the small house she shared with Doc. He'd be there, she knew he would. And he'd know what was wrong. Kate practically flew through the saloon's swinging doors and ran east on Allen Street. As she neared the corner she slowed, not able to believe what she was seeing . . . or rather, what she wasn't seeing. Where was the house? Kate looked around frantically. Sixth and Allen. This was it. She stared at the vacant lot where the house should have stood. Then she remembered. It had burned down, just a few weeks before, and she and Doc had taken a room at the Palace Hotel.

Kate looked around again. When she'd passed there the day before, on her way to visit Irene Giffo, the area had still been littered with the remains of burned buildings.

Now it was completely bare.

Confused, Kate turned and ran back to the Oriental.

"Oh, good, you came back," Marion said, smiling as Kate barged through the swinging doors.

Kate looked from Marion to Ringo. "Everything's gone," she said, then gasped as a thought struck her. So many changes, so many things missing. Maybe she was dead and hadn't been good enough to get into heaven, and maybe not bad enough for hell. Her gaze darted about frantically. Was this some kind of purgatory? Were these people . . . ghosts? She glanced at Ringo,

remembered the feel of his hand wrapping around hers
when he'd pulled her from the cactus garden, remembered the feel of his arms, so hard, hot, and strong. No,
he wasn't a ghost.

"So, it's settled, then," Marion said when Kate
didn't answer, "you're coming home with us."

Jack stared at his mother. It was settled all right, he
thought to himself. By next week he'd surely be living
in the psychiatric ward of Tucson's state hospital,
driven nuts by his own family.

Kate heard them talking, but she wasn't listening.
Her attention had been grabbed by a calendar hanging
on the wall near the bar. Turning away from Marion
and Ringo, she slowly walked across the room, lifting
her skirt and moving between the tables, her heart
beating a thunderous cadence in her chest, her gaze
never leaving the calendar. She was too afraid to move
faster for fear that what she was seeing was real, that
the impossible had happened, yet she was unable not to
continue forward for fear of realizing what she was seeing was not real and she was crazier than all of the
people she'd been encountering since the stage crash—
if there really had been a stage crash. Kate stopped
upon reaching the bar and, gripping its edge tightly,
stared at the calendar, her gaze boring into it, her mind
still trying desperately to deny that it was real. Swallowing hard, she tore her gaze from the numbers that
had to be another delusion and whirled toward Ringo.

"Where are we?" she asked, interrupting whatever
he was saying to Marion.

He looked up at her, surprised. "Where are we?" he echoed sarcastically.

"Jacky, be good," Marion scolded.

"Where are we?" Kate snapped, fear suddenly overriding any semblance of patience. "What is this place?"

"Tombstone," Jack said.

"Tombstone," Kate repeated. "Tombstone, Arizona?"

"Is there another?"

She ignored the barbed comment. "Is this . . . is this calendar right?" She felt hysteria threatening to overwhelm her and fought it down, praying she was just in the middle of a bad dream, or someone's foolish idea of a joke. "Is it"—she was having a hard time even saying it—"it's not really . . . I mean . . . is it really 1997?"

"Dammit, stop the games, would you?" Jack's eyes flashed black. "Or are you going to tell me it's supposed to be 1881 and you're a little out of your element?"

Kate suddenly wanted to cry. She wanted to scream. She wanted to lash out and smash Ringo over the head with a chair. But most of all she wanted someone to wake her up.

Just then Boozer walked up and rubbed against her leg.

"Jacky," Marion said excitedly, "maybe it's like in the movies. Maybe she was caught in an avalanche or something years ago and frozen alive, and she just woke up."

The room suddenly started to spin and blackness began to well up around Kate. She gripped the bar. No, she thought, she couldn't give in . . . she had to stay alert . . . find out what was happening . . . find Doc. . . .

"Oh, great," Jack snapped, lunging forward to catch her. He'd often dreamed of having a woman swoon at his feet, but he'd always hoped it would be because she was hot for him, not because she was half-nuts and he'd growled her head off and probably scared her silly.

FIVE

"You'll stay in this room tonight, dear." Marion ushered Kate into what she'd mentioned earlier was Jack's den. "Here are a pair of Liz's jeans and a shirt, and a few other things, in case you want to change."

Kate nodded absently and looked around, wondering again why she'd allowed herself to be brought back to this place. But she knew why. She didn't know what else to do, or where else to go. Something had happened when the stagecoach had crashed. Something she couldn't explain, something that, even thinking about it, frightened her beyond belief. She felt her hands begin to tremble again and clasped them together.

Marion picked up several newspapers that had been left on a table. "We're so glad you came, Kate," she said cheerily.

"Me too," Kate managed weakly. She was glad she'd come, because at the moment she was too confused to have done anything else, and Marion Ringo was the only person offering her any kind of refuge. She looked around the room. It was unusual, yet somehow, in a way she didn't understand, she could feel Ringo there, and in spite of herself and the fact that he'd so far treated her with nothing but coldness, that sense of him offered her comfort.

Two walls were covered with shelves, all crammed with books, and the weirdest settee she'd ever seen was set up against another wall. It was huge, with jagged slashes of red, green, white, and black and big pillows covered with the same fabric piled on top of it. Some kind of table was set against another wall and a gray box with a black window was set in its center. Little colored squares, like slanted windows with tails, were floating in the black square.

"I don't know why Jacky has to leave his computer on all the time," Marion said. She pushed a button and the little colored squares abruptly disappeared. "Now"—she turned to Kate—"dinner will be in about an hour. You relax for a while, and we'll make up the bed after dinner, okay?"

Kate wanted to say what bed?—but decided she'd wait until later. The older woman had probably just shown her to the wrong room. Her gaze fell on the papers Marion had collected and was still holding. "Are those newspapers?"

"Yes. Jacky never picks up after himself." Marion laughed. "If I didn't come in here at least once a week, he'd probably be buried in these things." She laughed again. "I can just see the headlines, 'Local businessman disappears . . . found days later in his study under stack of papers.' "

"Could I—" Kate's voice broke. She was still having a hard time believing what had happened. "Could you leave them?" she asked finally.

"The papers?" Marion's brows rose in surprise. "Well, of course, dear, if you like." She set them in front of the thing she'd called a computer. "But they're old, you know? I mean, most are from last week."

"That's all right," Kate said. "I'm . . ." She searched her mind for an explanation, then remembered the Englishman she'd met in Wichita who said he'd come to town to do research for a book he was writing on the West. "I'm doing some research," she said, "for a book."

"Oh, how interesting." Marion plumped the pillows on the huge settee. "Be sure to tell Jacky that. He writes, too, you know? For several magazines. When he's not tending to the saloon, that is. Stories about the military, new jet planes, flying, and things like that."

"Flying?" Kate echoed incredulously.

Marion waved a hand in the air. "Nothing I understand, mind you, but he loved the air force, until he had that accident." She shook her head and straightened several books on the shelf. "We almost lost him, but"—she turned and smiled brightly—"that's what brought him back home. He couldn't fly anymore, so he moved Cathy and the kids back here. Then"—the smile disappeared again—"Cathy died, poor thing. And he still misses her." She headed for the door. "But you tell Jacky about your book. He'll be real interested in that."

After Marion left, Kate picked up the papers. If she really had . . . if she really was in . . . Her mind tried to reject the possibility. She sat on the settee and spread the first paper out before her. An hour later she knew, beyond any doubt, that the impossible had happened, and that the man she'd thought was Johnny Ringo wasn't.

She should have known. He had been insufferable since the moment they'd met: grouchy, stubborn, mean-spirited, and downright rude. Not too different from Ringo, except with Ringo all of those traits had been expressed with a touch of deviltry. Yet as rigid and hard as Jack had been, she couldn't deny she felt drawn to him.

Kate popped to her feet, shoving the paper away. "This is ludicrous." She began to pace the small room. How could she be in 1997? That was the future, and the future hadn't even happened yet. She paused and looked down at the paper again, at the room with its weird furnishings, and then she saw the framed newspaper on the wall. Moving to stand before it, she read the headline, then the date of the paper's issue, and finally the story.

They were dead. Johnny, Curly Bill, Cactus Jack, Billy Clanton, Bob McLowery. She sighed deeply. It was true, then, she couldn't deny it anymore. She was in 1997. But how? Why? And what was she going to do? More importantly: Was there a way to get back?

The thought caused her breath to stop in her

throat. Back? Did she want to go back? Kate moved to the window and stared out at the desert. She'd been on a stagecoach under attack by Apaches when it had careened out of control and crashed. If she found a way back, would it be to that same time? That same moment?

Her gaze turned skyward. Was that it? Had she been saved from death by being flung into the future? Her racing heart suddenly calmed, and she felt an unusual peace settle over her. That was it. That had to be it.

Jack let out a long sigh, grabbed a towel from under the bar, and wiped his hands. He turned to his bartender. "Think you can hold down the fort by yourself, Ben? I've got something I want to do."

The older man, who'd worked the saloon with Jack during the festival for the last five years, nodded, and a stream of sunlight flowing into the room from above the entry's swinging doors danced off his bald pate. "Sure. Compared to what tomorrow will be like when the festival officially starts, today's most likely a piece of cake." He reached up and fingered the black handlebar mustache that had been waxed into a huge curl at each end.

Jack nodded. "Good. I'll be back in about half an hour." He crossed the street and headed down Fifth, wanting to avoid the tourists meandering from shop to shop on Allen Street. The festival wouldn't start until the next morning, but the crowds were already in attendance.

As he turned on Toughnut the old two-story courthouse came into view. If his mother wanted to pacify a nutcase and take her into their home, fine. He couldn't stop her. He'd never been able to stop her. Neither had his father. She was always taking in strays of one kind or another, and had for as long as Jack could remember. But this one was different. This one was either playing some sort of game with them, or playing at life with less than a full deck, and if he was going to do one thing when he got home, it was make her tell him the truth about who she was.

Hell, for all he knew they were harboring a wanted criminal.

Jack entered the courthouse and spotted Maggie Conley, the town's leading historian. He waved, urging her away from the tourists who were lingering about looking at the room's old relics and pictures.

"Hi, Jack, what's up?" she said, smiling.

"You got any pictures of Big-nosed Kate around, Maggie?"

Her already deeply lined brow furrowed into a road map of wrinkles. "Did you try the library?"

Jack shook his head. "I passed by there, but they're closed."

She shrugged. "We've got a lot of old pictures here, but I'm not sure about her. What do you need it for?" She walked toward a bookshelf on the other side of the room, gray-streaked brown hair bobbing on her shoulders.

Jack stared after her. What did he need it for? That was a good question. What was he supposed to say? That he needed it so he could force their houseguest to admit she wasn't a woman who'd lived in Tombstone a hundred and sixteen years ago? He suddenly felt like a fool.

"Ah, never mind, Maggie." He turned toward the door. "It's not important."

"Oh, look, we do have one," she called out. "I wasn't sure because there weren't any framed and on the wall."

He turned back, unable to stifle his curiosity.

"But I'm afraid it's not a very good one, Jack," Maggie said, holding it out to him. "I mean, the old posed, studio portraits they used to take were the best for clarity. This is a street scene."

Jack stared at the faded daguerreotype. Not very good was the understatement of the century. It looked like it had been taken on Allen Street, and if he wasn't mistaken, the building in the background was the Oriental. But the photo was grainy and slightly out of focus. Doc Holliday was barely recognizable, standing on the boardwalk in front of the saloon. A woman stood beside him, her face half in shadow, her arm linked through his. Jack stared hard, eyes narrowed in an effort to make out her features. But it was impossible.

He handed the photo back to Maggie. "Did Big-nosed Kate have any relatives, Maggie? Any family?"

"I don't think anyone really knows, Jack, and as I recall, no one ever heard of her before she took up with Doc, and when she left Tombstone she disappeared."

"Disappeared?"

Maggie nodded. "The stagecoach she took when she left town was attacked by Apaches. My great-great-uncle was the driver, you know." She smiled proudly. "Anyway, a whiskey salesman who was on the coach and claimed to have fallen out during the attack came back to town and told everyone what had happened. They rode out and found the coach a few days later at the bottom of a canyon. Hank Conley's body was there, shot full of arrows and missing his scalp, poor man, but they never did find Big-nosed Kate."

Jack stared at Maggie, recalling the story now and remembering Kate's words. Apaches. Stagecoach. Attack. He turned and slammed out of the courthouse, nearly knocking down several tourists in his haste to get outside. She was an actress, that was all, he told himself. Anyone who wanted to find out that information could do so. It was probably in dozens of books. Whoever the woman was, she was acting. Period. But the question was why. Why was she acting, and why had she picked on the Ringo family as an audience for her little charade?

He took his time walking back to the Oriental. Tonight after dinner he intended to ask their guest a few questions. Hard questions. And he wouldn't accept any silly "I'm Kate Holliday" answers either. If she was going to stay in *his* house, with *his* mother, and *his* daughters, then he wanted to know exactly who she was.

"Hey, boss," Ben called out the moment Jack stepped into the saloon. He moved away from the swinging doors and toward the bar. "LeeAnn was here looking for you a little while ago. Sullen as a sore-headed dog when she found out you weren't around too."

Jack nearly groaned. LeeAnn Clay was not what he needed at this moment. Or at any moment, for that matter. They'd dated casually for a while, or at least Jack had thought it was casual. He'd also thought Lee-Ann had understood that. For the last month, however, even though they hadn't had a real date, LeeAnn had begun to act extremely possessive, and Jack didn't like it. He'd tried to be a gentleman about it, since LeeAnn was his sister's best friend, and the mayor's daughter, but his patience and manners would only stretch so far. He was beginning to think the word to describe Lee-Ann wasn't actually possessive, but obsessive. "What'd you tell her, Ben?" he asked, nearly holding his breath.

"Said you'd headed up to the mountains for a few days to search for gold." Ben laughed. "Don't think she bought it, though. Left grumbling about how after you two got married, she'd see to it I wouldn't have a job here anymore."

Jack's smile was more a grimace. "Great," he snapped, the word sounding like a curse. LeeAnn was a nice woman, a beautiful, even desirable woman, but he wasn't in love with her, and he knew he never would be. He stalked his way behind the bar, which, since it was almost five o'clock and dinnertime, was nearly empty.

"You'd better find a way to cool that little she-cat

off," Ben said, "before her attraction to you turns kinda fatal. Y'know what I mean?"

Jack did know. He just didn't know what to do. Right from the start, from that first time Liz managed to talk him into going to dinner with LeeAnn, he'd tried to make certain she knew he wasn't looking for or interested in a serious relationship. And he'd thought she understood. Accepted it. He'd also tried to tell her that again a few weeks before, when she'd started hinting around about wedding rings and their future.

"Pretty interesting houseguest you picked up for yourself. Kate Holliday, huh?"

Jack caught the sly look that flashed onto Ben's face while the man smiled and tried to sound innocent. "My mother picked her up." He grabbed his hat from a hook behind the bar. "Think you can lock up tonight, Ben? I want to get home early."

Twenty minutes later he walked into familiar pandemonium.

Jessi had six kittens and five little girls in the family room.

KaraLynn was using the dining room as her own private roller rink, most likely courtesy of his mother.

And Tiffany and Liz were in the living room hunched over a coffee table and an ominous array of makeup.

"Tiff," Jack said, "no makeup."

She looked crushed. "But, Dad . . ."

"No. And I'll hang your aunt Liz if she dares to defy me on this and lets you use any of that stuff." He walked away from the doorway before his sister could

respond. His mother was probably in the kitchen with
their guest. Jack headed for his den, his retreat, the
only room in the house besides his bedroom that he
could actually call his own. His mother would call him
when dinner was ready. Until then he planned to sit
alone in his room at the rear of the house and think
about just what questions he was going to zing their
guest with. He opened the door.

Kate jerked upright with a gasp. Her fingers lost
their hold on the jeans she was trying to pull up over
her legs, and they fell in a faded blue pool around her
ankles.

Jack's gaze dropped to her bare legs, then traversed
their length like a skier flying over the perfect run, fast,
swift, and totally enraptured by the experience. When
his gaze finally made it back to the tails of the white
shirt hanging over a pair of pink silk-and-lace bikini
panties, he sucked in a deep breath.

Long, almost black hair spread across her shoulders
in thick, tangled waves, a rich, deep contrast to the
white not-yet-buttoned shirt and the sheer, beribboned
camisole beneath it, which left little to his imagination.

Kate watched him, felt her cheeks heat with the
flush of embarrassment, then tensed against the un-
wanted and unusual physical sensation. She had been
with Doc for a long time, long enough to get used to a
man looking at her with want in his eyes and need in
his blood. Indignation overrode the feeling of embarrassment. She was used to the look, but only when it
was invited, and his was not. She grabbed for the skirt
she'd tossed across a nearby chair.

Jack's gaze practically devoured her as she moved, and his body grew instantly hard and hot, even as his mind told him to apologize, back away, and close the door. But he couldn't move. She was too beautiful. Her skin was the creamy white of a saguaro blossom, her curves fashioned for the sweep of a man's hands, her body made for loving. She was a temptation he suddenly did not want to resist, the realization of all his fantasies, even ones he'd been unaware of. He wanted to scoop her into his arms, crush her body to his, and rake his hands over every inch of her until she cried out her need for him.

The hot, raw hunger Kate saw in Jack's eyes reminded her of Johnny, the look he'd given her that night Doc had— She pushed the thought aside and jerked the gown to her breasts, holding it there so that its voluminous folds concealed her half-naked body. This was not Johnny Ringo standing before her. This man was a stranger, a tall, dark stranger who was making her feel things she didn't want to feel, think about things she didn't want to think about. And no one made Kate Holliday do anything she didn't want to do.

She squared her shoulders and threw her chin up in defiance. "I don't usually allow just anyone to see me half-clothed, Mr. Ringo," she said, her tone dripping ice.

Jack smiled. "Only Doc?" he asked tauntingly.

Kate stared at him, taken aback. Was he saying he believed her?

"Or Johnny?" Jack added, his tone etched with soft sarcasm and biting challenge. He was playing a dangerous game, but suddenly it was exactly the kind of game he wanted to play with her. "I'm Johnny Ringo's great-great-great-grandson, Kate," he said, his eyes dark and riveted upon hers as he walked toward her. "Doesn't that count?"

She tensed as he neared then stopped before her, so close, she could feel the heat emanating from his body, reaching out to her, caressing her. She steeled herself against the urge to touch him, as if his mere presence was a magnet, pulling her.

His gaze moved to her mouth and lingered there, shockingly hungry, blatantly appraising.

Kate remained still, trying to ignore the wild rhythm that had begun to throb within her body. What was there about this man that sent her senses reeling? What was there about him that made her suddenly want him like she'd never wanted any other man?

He touched the tip of his index finger to her cheek, then let it skim down the length of her neck until it came to rest in the shadowed cleavage between her breasts.

Kate shivered at the intimately provocative touch. It was so light, barely discernible, and gentle, yet at the same time it was so seductive that it brought a groan from her lips and made her want to lean toward him, slip her arms around his neck, and pull him close.

Jack felt a rush of heat surge through his blood at her response, the sensation like fire sweeping over a barren floe of ice, melting everything in its path. Feelings coursed through him that he wasn't prepared to acknowledge, feelings that, since the death of his wife, he'd never thought to feel for another woman. Yet he reveled in them, enjoying without thinking.

Exerting every ounce of willpower she possessed, Kate raised a hand to his chest. She knew he intended to kiss her, and she knew she couldn't allow that. But suddenly his heartbeat was beneath her hand, pulsing, throbbing against her palm, the ancient aphrodisiac of a man's virility, a man's desire, calling to her.

Jack felt her touch like a brand of fire, burning into his flesh. He lowered his head and brushed a light kiss across her lips. "I want you," he whispered roughly, "and you know you want me."

What she wanted was to deny his words, deny him, but she couldn't move, could barely breathe for the swell of confusion—and the rush of desire—coursing through her. She had expected him to be rough, his kiss to be harsh, demanding, and savage, the way Johnny's had been that night so long ago. Instead, Jack's lips touched her with a tender power that was even more devastating, a gentleness that was more savagely conquering than any force she could imagine, any man's touch she had ever experienced.

His lips moved along the line of her jaw, then slowly returned to cover her mouth again, this time his kiss a little more demanding, a little more possessive. And this time she returned the caress, opening her mouth to his, welcoming the invasion of his tongue, the assault of his passion. A delicious, shivering warmth spread through her body, igniting something deep in the core of her being and invading every cell. Kate moved her hands up over Jack's strong arms and slipped hers around his neck.

He felt himself drowning in flames. He had jumped into the fire, and he was burning up. His hands went around her waist and dragged her up against him, crushing her body to his, pressing his hard sex against her stomach.

Kate melted against him, unconsciously leaning into him as the raging hunger he had awakened within her yearned to be satiated. His lips moved over hers hungrily, his arms held her tighter than she'd ever been held, his body pressed to hers until curve fit curve, and line melded with line. Need clawed its way through her blood.

Just as the need to possess and be possessed became almost more than she could bear, Jack's arms dropped from around her and he pushed away.

He turned abruptly, then as swiftly turned back and stared at her, his breathing ragged and harsh, a silver sheen of perspiration dampening his forehead.

Kate took a step back, dazed from his kiss, stunned by his abrupt termination of it. Her gaze rose and met his, and she suddenly wanted nothing more than to hide from the hard, angry look that sparked from his eyes.

"Who are you?" he demanded, his voice husky with emotion and dark with fury. "Just who the hell are you?"

SIX

She didn't want to face him again, experience the kind of feelings he seemed to ignite within her with just a look. Memory of his kiss sent a scorching heat racing through her veins.

Kate tried to ignore it, deny it, and looked around, trying to forestall the moment she would have to leave the security of this small room and walk down the hall to the dining room, where the others would be waiting.

Her gaze moved over the furnishings, the thing Marion had called a computer, and finally paused on the newspapers. The things she'd read had shocked and amazed her. This world was too complicated for her, there were too many things in it she didn't understand, too many things she knew she'd never be able to accept.

Like Jack Ringo, a little voice in the back of her mind whispered.

Every independent, defiant cell in Kate's body stiffened against the thought. She took a deep breath. It had only been a kiss. A simple, stolen kiss, and she was being foolish to give it any more significance. But she'd responded to it in a way she'd never have expected, in a way she never had to any other man: instantly, brazenly, with more heat and hunger than she'd thought possible.

"No." Since she hadn't meant to speak aloud, the sound of her own voice startled her. Kate moved to look through the window. Johnny had not only been an outlaw and a ruthless killer, he'd also been a notorious lothario, an out-an-out womanizer, and his descendant probably was too. Yet even as she thought it, something—maybe the fact that he lived with his mother, sister, and three daughters—told her she was wrong.

"Kate, dinner's ready." Marion's voice sang down the hall.

Kate closed her eyes and ordered herself to calm down. Her hands continued to tremble. This was ridiculous. She had stared down hired gunmen, dealt with miners who hadn't seen a woman in months, fought off hostile Indians, and evidently even traveled through time. She took a deep breath and reached for the doorknob. She could do this.

Something crashed against the door.

Kate jumped and jerked her hand back.

The door swung open.

"Gram said to come get you for dinner," KaraLynn said, poking her head into the room and hanging on to the doorknob as her Rollerblades threatened to roll out from beneath her.

Kate nearly fainted in relief to see the little girl's face instead of Ringo's. "Thank you," she managed.

She threw one last glance toward a small mirror that hung on the wall near a closet door. The denim trousers Marion had given her hugged her legs and hips like a second skin, and the shoes felt as if they were going to fall off her feet any moment, having no heels, no top, and no laces. She stepped into the hallway to follow KaraLynn to the dining room. There was no putting it off any longer. She rounded a corner, entered the room, and her gaze met his instantly.

Jack's eyes darkened dangerously, and Kate saw the invitation that glittered in those smoldering blue depths, betraying the desire he felt. He looked suddenly all too wicked, all too dangerous, and, to her chagrin, all too seductive.

Jack watched the emotions that danced across her face as she stared at him, and for some reason that he wasn't in the mood to figure out, her obvious discomfort gave him a flash of satisfaction.

But what he did understand, and didn't like, was the surge of desire that swept over him the minute she stepped into the room. The urge to step nearer to her, to touch her, was almost irresistible. In fact, he wasn't so certain that if his mother, sister, and daughters weren't in the room, he would resist.

He was a little surprised at the ungentlemanly notion. Not that he thought of himself as the ultimate gentleman, but he didn't normally have the urge to rip off a woman's clothes either.

Kate felt the breath in her lungs stall and her pulse

begin to race, and stiffened. He wanted her, but why did that seem to set her so off-balance? She'd encountered dozens of men who'd wanted her, and none of them had the effect on her that Jack Ringo's mere presence seemed to have. What she did know, however, was that her reaction to his desire was one she didn't welcome, one she had to get under control.

Abrupt awareness that the inseam of his jeans was threatening to cut off his circulation suddenly became the uppermost thought in Jack's mind. He turned toward the table. "Let's sit down," he grumbled.

Kate took the seat Marion motioned her to, thankful it was not next to Jack. Nevertheless, every time she looked up, her gaze seemed drawn toward him. Her stomach did a flip-flop, and she knew she would eat very little.

Not even five minutes after they'd settled down at the table, a knock on the front door brought Marion and the children's chatter to an abrupt halt.

Marion popped up from her chair. "I'll get it."

But there was no need. The front door slammed open and Kate looked up to see a woman with long white-blonde hair, dressed entirely in white, storm into the room.

"Jack Ringo, how dare you stand me up," LeeAnn Clay snapped. She stood, fists on hips, glaring at the back of his head.

Everyone, including Kate, turned to look at Jack. He set his fork down calmly and turned in his seat, but Kate saw the sudden clench of his jaw and sensed he was anything but calm. "Stand you up, LeeAnn?"

"You were supposed to have dinner with Daddy and me tonight, Jack, and we waited over an hour for you."

Jack evaded Kate's gaze, set his napkin on the table, and stood. "And when did I commit to this, LeeAnn?"

Her ice-blue eyes flashed fury as she flipped hair over her shoulder with an insolent jerk of her head. "When? I told that bartender of yours this afternoon, that's when," she said.

"Ben." Jack nodded, deciding he just might get his own version of the famous gunfight at the O.K. Corral going at the saloon tomorrow when Ben showed up for work. The man had probably been trying to do him a favor by conveniently forgetting this part of LeeAnn's conversation with him. Jack would have to explain to Ben that this kind of favor he could do without. "Well, I'm sorry, LeeAnn, I guess it slipped my mind, with handling all the preparations for the festival and all."

LeeAnn snorted and, as if she'd read his mind, said, "He didn't tell you, did he?"

Jack gently but firmly took hold of her arm and turned her around toward the foyer. "As I said, Lee-Ann, I'm sorry. Maybe another time." He nearly bit off his tongue the moment he spoke the words. Why in the hell had he said that? Going to LeeAnn's wasn't anything he wanted to do again, now or ever.

She slid her arm from his grasp and turned back to stare at Kate. "And who is she?" she demanded.

Jack saw the jealousy in her eyes, heard it in her tone, and knew he'd better find a way to get her out of that room before things got a whole lot worse. He didn't want his girls, and Jessi's five little friends, to see something like that. He tried to take her arm again. "Come on, LeeAnn."

Jack threw Liz a glaring glance. This is *your* friend, he hoped the look in his eyes conveyed, so get over here and help me get rid of her.

Liz merely smiled and helped herself to some potatoes.

Marion resettled herself in her chair. "Oh, LeeAnn, honey, how rude of us, this is Kate Holliday," she said, and turned to Kate. "Kate, dear, this is Liz and Jack's friend LeeAnn Clay. Her daddy is the mayor and owns one of the largest ranches in the county."

LeeAnn impaled Marion with her eyes. "*The* largest ranch," she corrected haughtily.

Kate smiled. She might be Liz and Jack's friend, but it was plain as day she was one of the rudest women Kate had ever encountered and also had her sights set on Jack Ringo. And she didn't like the fact that Kate was sitting at his dinner table. Kate felt an unexpected flash of satisfaction at the woman's jealousy. That surprised her. What shocked her was the fact that she was jealous too.

Kate finally found her voice. "It's nice to meet you, Miss Clay."

"Kate Holliday?" LeeAnn looked down at Kate, her eyes shining with contemptuous disbelief. "Like in Doc Holliday?"

Kate forced herself to remain smiling. "Yes."

LeeAnn's expression turned to one of disdain and dismissal, and she waved a hand through the air. "Well, I wouldn't say that's anything to be proud of."

Instantly furious, Kate opened her mouth to issue a sharp retort, but LeeAnn turned away.

She practically threw herself against Jack, her bottom lip dropping into a pout, her arms encircling his neck.

Marion leaned toward Kate and touched her arm. "LeeAnn's family, on her mother's side, is descended from the Clantons," she whispered, "and to this day they've got a grudge against the Earps and their friends."

Kate felt like turning to LeeAnn and saying, Well, being descended from the Clantons is nothing to be proud of, but she remained silent.

"Come into town with me tonight, Jack," LeeAnn cooed suggestively. "We could have a couple of drinks and"—she shrugged and smiled—"whatever."

Jack felt eleven sets of eyes boring into his back like lasers. He fought to hang on to his patience and manners. LeeAnn's obsessiveness was getting out of hand. Why in blazes he'd ever let Liz talk him into going out with her in the first place, he'd never know. He took her by the arm and practically propelled her toward the front door. "LeeAnn, I had"—he glanced over his shoulder at Kate—"an unusual day today. I'm bushed, Jessi has company who don't need to see this, and I have a lot of paperwork to do tonight to get ready for the festival tomorrow. So I'll see you later."

LeeAnn lazed against the doorjamb. "Tonight?"

"No."

"Who's that woman?" she demanded, her tone suddenly hard and cold.

The woman I want. The thought shocked Jack so much, he stood silent for a moment, staring at LeeAnn, dumbfounded.

"Jack," LeeAnn snapped, jerking him back to the moment. "Who is that woman?"

"My mother's friend." It wasn't a lie, but it definitely wasn't the entire truth either. "Good night, LeeAnn," he said tiredly as he showed her to her car.

The house was quiet. Everyone had gone to bed except Jack. He roamed about the family room, trying to get his turbulent thoughts under control. He had too much to do in the upcoming days to be worrying about a woman who kept insisting she was Kate Holliday. And somehow he had to find a way to cool Lee-Ann's ardor.

"Jacky?"

He stopped his pacing and turned at his mother's voice.

She stood in the doorway, holding her fuzzy blue robe closed around her, a deep frown creasing her brow. She looked worried and about ready to cry, and that wasn't at all like Marion Ringo. Jack felt a flash of fear.

"What's wrong, Mom?"

She shuffled across the room. "Oh, Jacky, I don't know what to do. I can't find my gold earrings anywhere. You know, the ones your father gave me just before he"—her voice broke and she teared up—"you know . . . just before he died."

Jack's fear vanished, and he slipped an arm around her shoulders. "You probably just put them down somewhere and don't remember where. They'll turn up."

She shook her head. "No. I'm real careful with those earrings, Jacky, you know that. They're the last gift your dad gave me." She turned to stare through the open French doors. "I remember I had them on this afternoon when I went to town, and when I got back home my ear was bothering me, so I took them off. I was on my way outside to water my plants, and I put the earrings on the table in the foyer. But they're not there now, and the girls swear they haven't seen them."

"They'll turn up, Mom," Jack assured her. "Now, come on, go back to bed. You probably moved them and just don't remember."

She shook her head. "Your father will never forgive me if I've lost those earrings," she said, her voice again threatening to break.

SEVEN

Kate stared at herself in the mirror again, but this time instead of denims hugging her legs as if they'd been painted on, she was in what Marion had said were a pair of Liz's pajamas. They were soft, fuzzy feeling, and had pictures all over them of the weirdest orange-and-black-striped cat Kate had ever seen. And they were huge, making her feel as if she had on a giant's clothes. She climbed into bed, which only minutes before had been the settee, or couch, as Marion had called it, and closed her eyes.

Within no time she knew that sleep was not going to come anytime soon. Too many things were buzzing around in her head, too many unanswered questions, too many new experiences. But most of all, crowding out every other thought, was the image of Jack Ringo. It just wouldn't go away, his face hovering in her thoughts constantly, haunting her, teasing, reminding her of the past, and of an unknown future.

And now there was LeeAnn Clay. Kate didn't want to think about her, didn't want to feel the jealousy she'd felt the moment the woman had thrown herself into Jack's arms. She had been jealous of some of the women who'd thrown themselves at Doc, too, but it had never felt so strong, so overpowering, and she'd been with Doc for years!

Throwing aside the covers, Kate rose and crossed the room toward the glass doors that led to a gallery that wrapped almost entirely around the house. Hesitating, she reminded herself that there were no more savage Indians roaming the desert, no wild cowboys or ruthless outlaws to be wary of, then opened the French doors and stepped outside, breathing deeply of the desert's cool night air and feeling it envelop her. Moving to the edge of the gallery, she paused and stared up at the black sky. It was the same sky she'd always looked up at, the same moon, same stars. The same, yet so different now. A different time, different world. But why? she wondered. Why had this happened to her? For what purpose?

Jack lay in his bed and stared through the darkness at the ceiling. He'd tried to work on his books and found he couldn't concentrate. Thoughts of Kate kept intruding, distracting him until he finally gave up. He wanted her. He'd admitted that to himself already, but he had also determined that he wasn't going to do a damned thing about it. She was not only a stranger, she was just plain strange. She still insisted her name was

Kate Holliday, still acted as if she was unused to everything around her, and that made him uneasy.

The refrigerator seemed to frighten her. The microwave had made her eyes widen so much, he'd thought they were going to pop out of their sockets. And the car . . . the car terrified her.

He tried to push the thoughts aside, closed his eyes, and attempted to count sheep. When he reached one hundred and fifty, he gave up, still wide-awake, and lay still, listening to the house, or rather to its silence. Only late at night, when all the girls were asleep, did such silence visit the Ringo house.

Throwing aside the sheet, he rose, slipping on the pajama bottoms he rarely wore, but that his mother never failed to lay out for him, and ignoring the robe that she also always placed nearby. He couldn't sleep, he couldn't work, because Kate was in his den, and he didn't feel much like reading or watching television. Crossing the room, Jack jerked open the French doors, letting the desert night sweep into the room. The cool air felt invigorating, which was really the last thing he needed at the moment. Nevertheless, he stepped outside and walked barefoot to the edge of the gallery, then looked up. The moon was barely a sliver of gold in a sky so black, the stars looked like sparkling diamonds. It had been a long time since he'd met a woman who stirred his thoughts so thoroughly, and his body remained on alert even when she wasn't near.

Kate, standing beside one of the short, squat stucco pillars that supported the overhanging roof, sensed a movement to her left and tensed. She turned cautiously, afraid of who might be there in the darkness.

Standing only a few yards away, bathed in the soft glow of the summer moon, Jack Ringo was a startling contrast of light and shadow. His bronzed body, tall, lean, and hard, shone golden from the night light's touch, while darkness danced within each crevice of muscle, and moonbeams hid within the rich chestnut waves of his hair.

Kate knew she should go back to her room, but she hesitated to move, afraid it would draw his attention. She stood still, watching him, and suddenly, as if he'd felt her gaze upon him, he turned and walked toward her.

"I couldn't sleep," he said softly. *Because of you,* his eyes told her, before he tore his gaze away from hers and looked out at the night-shrouded desert.

A flowing warmth suddenly moved through Kate. It was a sensation that made her feel all too good, and one she didn't welcome. But her resistance was not strong enough to force her to move away from him. She looked up at his profile. "She's in love with you, you know."

Jack turned and looked down at her. "I know."

Kate nodded and started to turn away.

Jack reached out and laid a hand on her arm, a featherlight touch that sent shivers sweeping over her.

Kate paused and looked back at him.

His hand slid up her arm and his head lowered toward hers.

She knew she should back away, yet she remained still.

Unlike the kiss he'd stolen earlier, this one was soft and gentle, almost experimental. That was Kate's undoing, his hesitancy, the innocence and question in the caress of his lips.

She made no effort to resist, even as she fought against the desire welling up within her. The touch of his lips sent a wash of pleasure coursing through her, so intense, so achingly blissful, that her entire body stiffened in reaction.

His hand slipped around her waist and he moved closer, pulling her to him, closing the space between them.

She didn't want this, didn't need the complication in her life right now, but pushing him from her was more than she could do. Her will was gone, fear and caution vanquished, and all that was left was yearning . . . desire . . . need . . . for Jack Ringo.

His mouth moved over hers insistently, his kiss becoming a little more demanding, a little more seductive, coaxing her to respond, tempting her, daring her. And Kate Holliday had never been one to resist either pleasure or challenge.

She rose on tiptoes, slipping her arms around his neck, curling her fingers into the chestnut strands that curled about his nape.

Jack's embrace tightened at her response to his kiss, his lean body like a bulwark against the tempest of emotion that assaulted her. His kiss deepened, a moan of pleasure ripped from his throat, and passion, white-hot, fiery, and demanding, seized him mercilessly within its grip. He eased his tongue into her mouth, probing deeply, tasting ecstasy, and demanding rapture.

She answered with an invasion of her own, sensuously stroking his tongue with hers, plundering his already frayed emotions with each seductive answer to his lure.

Jack knew that what he had started, what he was doing, was wrong. But it didn't matter. Not now. He wanted her, had wanted her from the first, in a way he hadn't wanted a woman in a long, long time. He wanted to possess her, body and soul. To make her belong to him in a way she had never belonged to any other man. He wanted to fill her thoughts, her needs, and desires so that he was all she thought about, all she wanted.

Jack pushed Kate's back against the pillar, imprisoning her there as his kiss deepened, demanding and cajoling, tempting her further into a world of passion he knew neither of them should enter, and neither could resist. His intentions were not conscious. He was only conscious of Kate, of her soft, yielding, responding lips, the long, slim length of her legs pressed against his own, and her breasts—nipples pressing into his bare chest through the thin fabric of her pajamas. His body was afire, searing his veins, burning him from the inside out, as passion pooled in his groin like an inferno.

He slid his hands to the curve of her waist and held

her to him, his arousal telling her how badly he wanted
her, how badly he needed her.

Longing had never erupted so fiercely within his
body, need had never felt so desperate. When her arms
tightened around him, and he felt her responding, felt
her lips move from his and trail down his neck, down
the front of his chest, Jack growled low in his throat
and shuddered with want. Desire seized his body,
threatened to banish what little was left of his sanity,
and sever the thin thread he still maintained on his
control.

For the moment nothing mattered to him but the
woman in his arms, that the dark magic enveloping
them continue.

His kiss invoked an intimacy between them that
was greater than any Kate had ever experienced. Her
senses reeled under the burning pressure of his touch,
and a series of shivers ripped through her body. When
his hand moved to cup her breast, Kate arched into his
touch, wanting more, needing more, the desire he
aroused in her destroying any control she had left over
herself.

He continued to kiss her hungrily, devastatingly,
inflaming all the passions she had held in check since
the day she'd had to admit to herself that she was no
longer in love with Doc.

She felt Jack's hands, warm and vibrant, on her
body, awakening a heated sensitivity and a hunger so
raw and strong, she knew it had to be dealt with, had to
be satisfied, or she would explode.

No one had kissed her this way before, no one had

stirred her passions so intensely that nothing else mattered, and without doubt, she knew that no one ever would again. This was why she had been spared death. This was why she had traversed the world of time and come here . . . to him.

Suddenly, without reason or explanation, sanity slammed down on Kate so swiftly, it caused her entire body to tense. She shoved her hands between their bodies and, pressing against Jack's chest, pushed at him.

He drew away from her and stepped back, his breathing ragged against the silent night, desire blazing from his eyes, gripping every sinewy muscle of his body. A deep frown cut into his brow as his gaze bored into hers.

"That was a mistake," Kate said, her voice stirred by the emotions churning through her, the fire that had control of her. "I'm . . ." She shook her head and moved away, turning her back to him. A tear slipped from the corner of one eye, and she quickly blinked, destroying any evidence of her traitorous emotions.

She didn't really know this Jack Ringo, yet she knew everything about the other, and because of that, she knew he deserved better than she could ever give him.

EIGHT

She had let him get too close the night before, and she owed it to both of them to make certain it didn't happen again, that the attraction between them went no further. It didn't matter that every cell in her body wanted him to love her, ached to have him drag her into his arms and hold her close, take her to his bed. She didn't know him, and she didn't know his world. At any moment she could be whisked away as abruptly as she'd been plopped down in his garden.

Kate straightened her shoulders and looked past the saloon's swinging doors at the empty street. Everything was so different now. Would she ever get used to this time? This life? Or would she even be there long enough for that?

"The tourists will be arriving in about an hour," Jack said.

Kate turned and looked at him. He stood behind the bar, setting out clean glasses and rechecking his

stock to make certain everything was ready for the festival crowd. She forced herself to smile and nod. It
would be all too easy to fall in love with Jack Ringo,
but she wouldn't . . . couldn't let that happen.

He had loved one woman already. Marion had told
her about his wife, and what Jack had gone through
when she died. He didn't deserve to go through that
kind of pain again, and Kate knew that if she let this
thing that was between them get out of hand, if she let
him start having feelings for her, pain might just be all
too real a possibility for Jack.

The festival officially started that morning, so Jack
was in costume, and seeing him like that had nearly
taken Kate's breath away and made her, for just a moment, wonder if she'd been transported back to her
own time without realizing it. Then he'd asked her a
question, and she'd known it was Jack, not Johnny,
staring out from beneath the black Stetson that settled
a veil of shadow over his eyes, slightly obscuring the
wicked gleam she was beginning to realize was always
there. But there was no cruelty in Jack's eyes, as there
had been in Johnny's.

A holster rode low on his hips, and she recognized
the guns that were sheathed within the worn leather,
the curved, polished wooden handles, a series of
notches carved into them. They were Johnny's guns.

Jack Ringo was the image of Johnny, but never
more so than today. A shiver skipped up Kate's back,
and even though she knew better, she glanced at the
door, suddenly afraid she would see Doc standing
there, ready to call Jack down, ready to draw on him,

kill him. She forced the thought away, knowing it was ridiculous, and approached the bar, still undecided whether Marion's idea for her to work at the saloon had been a good one. It meant she'd be around Jack all day, which was like a forbidden euphoria, something part of her wanted, while the other part knew it was wrong. But after Kate had insisted on doing something to pay her for their generosity, she hadn't been able to offer a reason why working at their saloon wasn't the best solution. Especially since she didn't have anything with which to pay them.

At least it would give her time to acquaint herself more with this new world. And she'd feel safe in the Oriental, and *be* safe . . . if she stayed away from Jack. She more than knew her way around a bar, knew how to make a drink, deal a deck of cards, and make a man smile. Those, she assumed, were things that hadn't changed in the last hundred and sixteen years.

"What would you like me to do?" Kate asked.

Jack shrugged. "You could take the chairs down from the tables and set them up. Other than that, there's not much action till people start arriving."

Kate moved to a table near the rear of the room and pulled down a chair. "This was Doc's table," she said, not even aware she'd spoken aloud.

"That was Wyatt's table," Jack countered coolly.

Kate shook her head. "No. Wyatt liked to deal from that table over there, where he could see everyone." She pointed to one nearer the wall.

Jack sneered and leaned on the bar, his gaze raking

over her contemptuously. "You mean Doc and Wyatt, supposed best friends, didn't play at the same table?"

"Not if they were playing serious," she said, not noticing the derision in his tone. Kate stared at the table as if she could almost see the men she was talking about, dealing their cards, flinging their greenbacks and golden eagles into the center of the table. She looked up at Jack. "What would have been the point? It was the miners' money they wanted, not each other's."

"And sitting at different tables, they could run two different poker games, right?"

"Yes."

Jack grabbed several glasses from a shelf and slammed them down into place on the bar. "Boy, lady, you are good," he snapped. "Any more little tidbits of history you'd like to share? Like how Doc Holliday killed so many people and never got charged with murder? I mean, I'm sure you could correct a lot of the stories people tell around here about those days. Maybe even rewrite some of our history books."

She'd done it again, Kate realized. A series of curses stomped through her mind. Every time she mentioned the past or Doc, Jack became cold and angry. She'd promised herself that she wouldn't do it again, but it wasn't easy. It had been her life, dammit, and it was only natural during a conversation to refer to things that had happened and people she'd known.

"Good morning, Jack, honey."

LeeAnn Clay stood in the doorway, dressed for the festival.

Kate unconsciously bristled at the smile that came to Jack's lips as his gaze settled on LeeAnn.

He walked around the bar and approached her.

Kate did a quick assessment of LeeAnn's attire and bit her lower lip to keep from laughing. Her long gown was white—didn't the woman wear any other color?—and since the festival was supposed to be a celebration of the 1880s, Kate assumed the outfit was meant to be the height of fashion for that time. But the bodice hugged LeeAnn's breasts like a man's hands, and a "lady" would never wear anything like that. Her décolletage was so scandalously low, even Kate was shocked, and some of her "working" gowns had revealed plenty. Large puffed white sleeves covered Lee-Ann's shoulders, and instead of a flounced skirt and bustle, her skirt hugged her derriere, bustleless, and flared out below the knees.

It was so tight, Kate wondered how she could walk.

Her white-blonde hair was arranged in a mass of sausage curls that coiled down one side of her neck, and a wide-brimmed white hat adorned with feathers and silk flowers covered her head.

"LeeAnn," Jack said, "your costume is beautiful."

Kate nearly scoffed.

"Thank you, Jack," LeeAnn cooed, moving closer and brushing against him so that one breast caressed his arm. She ignored Kate and looked up at Jack suggestively. "I just wanted to stop by and show you my costume and see if you'd have lunch with me today. Maybe after your shoot-out thing."

Kate frowned. Shoot-out thing?

Jack shook his head. "I don't think so, LeeAnn. Sorry. We're going to be pretty busy here at the saloon, and I doubt I'll have a free minute."

A pouty little smile tugged at her lips. "Aren't you scheduled to have two shoot-outs today, Jack?"

He nodded. "Yeah. One at noon, the other at two."

"Well"—her smile turned coy, the look in her eyes mischievous—"since the sheriff today is my daddy, I'll just tell him you can't do that little ol' shoot-out at noon 'cause you'll be with me. They can get someone else, or cancel it altogether."

Kate purposely cleared her throat.

LeeAnn peered around Jack's shoulder. "What's *she* doing here?"

"Working," Jack said.

Kate smiled and waved, feeling a swell of satisfaction at seeing LeeAnn glare. "Good morning, Miss Clay."

LeeAnn sniffed, flapped the feather-tipped fan she held in one hand, and smiled slyly. "Miss Holliday."

Kate felt the woman's gaze rake over her like a five-pronged pitchfork.

"You certainly do look right at home in that outfit," LeeAnn said.

Kate's temper flared instantly. She knew an insult when she heard one, even when it was sugarcoated in flattery. And especially since, if she had been home, she never would have been caught dead in the gown Jack had given her to wear. The satin was an outrageous red, and the short ruffled sleeves, knee-length, full skirt with a ruffle at the hemline, and a large bow at the back of her tightly cinched waist was more the style of the lower-class saloon girls than something Kate would ever have worn. And the black fringe trim on the skirt had gone out of style long before she'd even arrived in Tombstone with Doc.

"It fits you so well, dear," LeeAnn continued. "Like it was made for you."

Kate stormed up to the woman. "It's a costume, Miss Clay," she snapped, "a poor one, and an insult to the elegant gowns I wore when I was here with Doc. And you obviously don't even have the good taste to know it. Or"—her gaze swept over LeeAnn's gown— "what was actually fashionable then."

LeeAnn gasped and stared at Kate as if she was crazy.

Ignoring LeeAnn, Jack grabbed Kate by the arm and steered her to his office in the back of the saloon, not caring that she practically had to run to keep up with him. Slamming the door behind them, he released her so suddenly, she stumbled.

"What in the hell is the matter with you?" he growled. "My family has offered you every hospitality, every consideration, even a job, and you continue to play this damned game of yours, talking about the past as if you were really in it."

"I was," Kate snapped.

"Yeah, maybe in your mind," Jack countered, "the sanity of which I'm beginning to have serious doubts about."

"I don't care what you think, Jack Ringo." Kate stomped across the room, then turned to glare at him, too angry even to consider her words. "I'm Kate Holliday, and the one thing I've never done is lie. I was on a stagecoach, leaving Tombstone, when it was attacked by Indians and crashed. The next thing I knew I was lying on the ground and you were standing over me griping about your damned cactus garden."

"Stop the games, Kate"—Jack closed the space between them and glowered down at her—"or whatever your name really is."

Her hand swung toward his cheek.

Jack's shot up and caught her arm, his strong fingers curling about her wrist. "*That's* not a good idea," he said with a snarl.

She swung out with her other hand.

He caught it, then pushed her backward, crushing her against the wall with his body, pinning her arms above her head. They'd been in this position before, and he knew how dangerous it was, knew that being this close to her was like fighting bare-handed with fire. He'd lost the battle the last time, and he knew he was going to lose it again. "Dammit," he growled huskily, "what the hell is it about you that drives me nuts?"

Kate stared up at him, her breath ragged, her pulse speeding. But before she could answer, before she could attempt to twist free, his mouth came down on hers, and the will to get away from him vanished.

The night before a thread of hesitancy had been in his kiss, an innocence and caution that had aroused tenderness and question. There was none of that this time. This kiss demanded her surrender, savagely commandeered her will. It was a deliberate assault on her senses that incited hot, hungry emotions that refused to be ignored.

She made a small attempt at escape, but it was only halfhearted, and they both knew it.

Feeling her resistance, Jack tightened his hold on her wrists, keeping her his prisoner when she secretly had no desire to escape. His hard length pressed against hers, line for line, curve for curve, fire igniting fire, yearning to meld, to blend into one.

He kissed her for a long time, an eternity during which Kate learned the depths of her own hungers and feelings. No one had ever kissed her like that before, so savagely, demanding her acquiescence while conquering her soul. A tiny moan escaped from her mouth into his as an unexpected but pleasurable ache suddenly hit her loins.

His caressing lips drained away her anger and replaced it with a burning need. She wanted to hold him to her, to wrap her arms around his neck, slip her fingers into the gold-tinged darkness of his hair. But he refused to release her arms, and all she could do was press her body to his.

His mouth moved from hers, and he covered her face and throat with a series of kisses, urgent and demanding.

Kate shuddered as another wave of desire coursed through her. She was losing control and she didn't care. At any moment she would give in to the swirling ache of desire that was attacking her body, that had been raging within her since the first moment she'd seen him. She wanted him. Needed him. And damn the consequences. Kate opened her eyes, needing to look into those midnight-blue eyes. Instead her gaze fell on the old portrait tacked up on the opposite wall, and she froze.

Johnny Ringo stared down at her, a smug smile curving his lips and a look of amusement in his eyes.

"No." As Kate tried to twist away from Jack, desire suddenly turned to anguish. "Please, stop."

Jack broke away from her abruptly, released her arms, and took a step back. His eyes blazed with passion, but realization and disbelief swept over him swiftly as he stared down at her. "I know," he said, his tone ragged with fury, "that was a mistake."

"No, I . . . ." She saw the hurt in his eyes and wanted to explain, wanted him to know why she couldn't let this thing between them go any further. But what could she say? He didn't believe the truth, and maybe that was best, because in spite of everything, Kate still wasn't certain she truly believed it either.

He turned on his heel, raking a hand through his hair, then grabbed the Stetson he'd slammed down onto his desk and stalked to the door. Jerking it open, he nearly tripped over Boozer. Cursing, he turned back to Kate. "You're right, lady, it was a mistake"—he paused as his words hung in the silence of the room—"and you can be damned sure it won't happen again."

NINE

The day had proven to be one of the longest and most unusual of Kate's life. Jack had remained aloof toward her, which she'd tried—in vain—to convince herself was for the best. His bartender had reminded her so much of Wyatt's bartender, she'd accidentally called him Frank several times. At least the dozens of people who'd come in and out of the saloon had been fascinating.

By late afternoon, Kate was exhausted, but Marion, Liz, and the girls had come by and insisted she not only join them at Nellie Cashman's restaurant for a late lunch, but also for the parade afterward.

Nellie's place didn't look anything like it had when Nellie was there, but the food was good. When Kate tried to bow out of going to the parade, saying she was tired, Marion clucked like a mother hen and insisted that Kate just couldn't miss the parade.

Jack had remained silent.

Kate stared at the riders moving down the street before her. Their outfits shone in the light of the setting sun, their saddles dripped with silver, and their horses were the most beautiful creatures she'd ever seen.

In startling contrast, several clowns, faces painted garishly, pranced about tossing candy to the children. A bevy of what Kate assumed were saloon girls, barely half-clothed and their faces overly painted, rode past in a buckboard, laughing and throwing kisses to the people crowding the boardwalk. An old prospector and his mule trudged past, grumbling softly and ignoring everyone.

But it was the four men moving side by side behind the prospector, their black long coats flapping about their knees as they walked, guns riding low on their hips, and hats pulled down to block out the sun, that drew and held Kate's attention and sent a stab of melancholy through her heart like a sharp knife. She stared as they passed, knowing full well that it wasn't Wyatt, Virgil, Morgan Earp, and Doc she was seeing, yet their presence was so real to her, so poignant still, that the sight of these costumed men nearly brought tears to her eyes.

"The mighty heroes," Jack murmured.

Kate turned sharply and stared up at him, hearing the rancor in his voice but seeing none of it on his face.

"Jack, darling, I've been looking everywhere for you," LeeAnn suddenly said, gushing as she wiggled between Kate and Jack. LeeAnn slipped her arms around one of Jack's and hugged it close, then stood on tiptoe to plant a kiss on his cheek. As she did this she slid one arm around his neck. "I thought we were going to meet in front of the Birdcage and watch the parade from there."

Jack looked down at her, trying to squelch the annoyance that had erupted in him the moment he'd heard her voice. LeeAnn was his sister's best friend, which most likely should have warned him not to go out with her. Her father was the town mayor, head of the restoration committee, and a member of almost every other committee. Everybody loved Sam Clay, but Jack had heard rumors of what had happened to a few people who'd gotten on his bad side. Jack didn't want to lose Sam's friendship, but he wasn't going to string LeeAnn along just to please her father. She was a nice person, but he wasn't in love with her. Hell, he wasn't even in lust with her.

But he was a gentleman, at least he tried to be, and at the moment he was straining to act accordingly. He reached up and removed LeeAnn's arm from his shoulders and turned to her. "LeeAnn, I told you when you came by the shoot-out this afternoon that I was going to be here with the girls, Mom, and Liz."

"You didn't say anything about *her*." LeeAnn glared at Kate.

"Kate is our guest at the ranch," Jack said, irritated at LeeAnn's tone and feeling a flash of protectiveness toward Kate that he didn't relish feeling, "naturally she was invited to join us."

"Well, sugar, they wouldn't miss you for a little while." LeeAnn slid a hand up and down Jack's arm.

One of the riders passing by called out to Jack, who turned and waved.

"LeeAnn, I really . . ."

Anger flashed in her eyes. "But I reserved us a table at the Lace Curtain for after the parade—" LeeAnn suddenly caught herself, reined in her tantrum, and pressed up against Jack again. "A nice, quiet table," she whispered, "way in the back." Her eyes flashed suggestively.

He was about to decline again when an idea occurred to him. "Good," he said. "I'll meet you there after I take the girls home." He'd make LeeAnn realize there was no future for them if it was the last thing he ever did.

"I can drive us all home," Liz offered, smiling up at her brother. "You can go ahead and go with LeeAnn now."

"And what do I do later," Jack said, "walk home?"

"Well, LeeAnn can drive you"—Liz's smile turned sly—"*if* you come home, that is."

Kate suddenly felt as if there was one woman too many standing in the company of Jack Ringo, and she was that woman. Turning away, she slipped into the crowd and made her way down the boardwalk, knowing that, having changed back into the jeans and shirt Liz had loaned her, and wearing her long hair brushed and flowing loose down her back, she would easily blend in.

A T-shirt store drew her attention, and she paused

to look in its window, her gaze moving over all the different-colored shirts, each with a saying or picture imprinted on it having to do with Tombstone, Wyatt, Doc, or Indians. Each one amazed her. Next she browsed through a jewelry store, marveling at the turquoise-and-silver jewelry the clerk swore was made by local Indians. If anyone had ever told Kate that a white woman would wear Indian jewelry, she'd have laughed. But that had been another lifetime.

Coming to the corner, she paused and looked in the window of a bookstore. A picture of Wyatt caught her eye. Going inside, Kate picked up the book and began to flip through it, then paused as a thought occurred to her. If she was suddenly sent back, would she want to know what had happened to everyone? She put the book down, then paused again. But what if she wasn't sent back? What if she stayed here? Then it was important to know. She picked the book back up and started looking for a page with a date later than the day she'd left Tombstone on the stage.

Suddenly her own name, written in big bold letters, caught her eye. She paused to read the words below it. Two paragraphs later she started in surprise.

> *On August 15, 1881, Big-nosed Kate, Doc Holliday's mistress, boarded a stagecoach bound for Tucson. The coach was attacked by Apache Indians about a half hour's ride from town.*
>
> *Two days later Henry Simmons, a whiskey salesman who claimed he was thrown off the ill-fated coach when it crashed, staggered into town. Sheriff*

Behan and several of his men rode out to the spot Simmons indicated and found the remains of the stage, which had evidently been forced over a cliff by the attacking Apaches. The driver was also found, several arrows in his body and his scalp missing. The horses were gone, and so was Big-nosed Kate.

It was assumed the attackers had taken her, as they had the horses and Hank Conley's scalp, but several Apaches who were caught a few days later swore the woman on the stage simply "vanished."

No one ever heard from Big-nosed Kate again.

No one ever heard from Big-nosed Kate again. The words echoed through her mind. Did that mean she never made it back? That she would stay here in 1997? She felt her hands tremble. Fear . . . or excitement? she wondered. She began to flip pages again.

"Can I help you, miss?"

Kate looked up at the young clerk. "No, ah, I just want to look at this book."

He nodded and went back to the magazine he'd been reading.

Kate returned to the book in her hands. A picture of a stable was on the page before her, the name O.K. Corral on a sign above the entrance. Kate recognized it and smiled, then dropped her gaze to the caption: *Scene of the shoot-out between the Earps and Doc Holliday and the Clanton–McLowery gang.*

The blood in her veins nearly turned to ice. Kate swallowed hard, her mouth suddenly dry. She remembered having seen the sign back at the store, the one she'd thought was Jeb Baker's cabin, next to the cemetery, but somehow it hadn't really registered, what with everything else that had happened.

Turning the page quickly, she scanned the words as a silent prayer sped through her mind. Finally, she released the breath she hadn't been aware she'd been holding. They had survived. Wyatt, Virgil, Morgan, and Doc. Virgil and Morgan had been wounded, but they'd all survived.

Now she couldn't stop reading. A moment later the peace she'd felt at learning that the Earps and Doc were safe turned to anguish, and she nearly burst into tears as she read how, in separate ambushes, Morgan had been murdered and Virgil left crippled. "Doc," she whispered frantically, flipping the pages. "What happened to Doc?"

"Excuse me?" the store clerk said, looking up at her.

Kate shook her head. "Nothing," she said. "Nothing."

She skimmed several more pages.

Wyatt had become a U.S. marshal, and fueled by a need for vengeance, he'd gone after Curly Bill, Ringo, Ike Clanton, and the rest of the Cowboys, with Doc and several others at his side.

Kate found a chair and sat down, fearing that she might faint.

No one was certain who killed Johnny Ringo, but according to the book, Doc had feigned being too sick to go on, telling Wyatt his tuberculosis was finally getting to him. But when Wyatt rode after Ringo, Doc did, too, and Doc got there first. He and Ringo faced off, and Ringo ended up dead.

Kate gasped and tears again stung her eyes, but whether they were tears of joy because Doc had survived, or tears for Johnny because he had not, she wasn't sure.

She set the book back on the display shelf and stood. The story of Doc and Johnny's confrontation had never been proven, but it was the kind of thing Doc would have done for Wyatt. She'd seen Ringo draw once, and knew he'd been faster than Wyatt. Wyatt would never have let Doc take on his fight, but doing it the way the book described, Kate knew, was just Doc's style.

Turning away, she was about to leave the bookstore when she paused. Whether she stayed in this strange new world she'd been tossed into, or was jerked out of it and thrown back into her own, she had to know one more thing.

Picking up the book again, she hurriedly flipped past the pages that had described Wyatt and Doc's chase after Curly Bill and Ringo until she came to the section she'd been seeking.

Three years after that ride, Doc checked himself into a sanitarium in Colorado and, after a visit by Wyatt, who proved to be his best friend right up to the end, quietly died of tuberculosis.

Kate set the book down and walked out of the store, tears streaming from her eyes. She made her way blindly down the boardwalk, instinctively heading for the Oriental Saloon, the only place in this "new" Tombstone that still felt like home to her.

"Kate?"

She stiffened. Instinct told her to run. She didn't want to see Jack now. Didn't want him to see her. She needed time to digest what she'd just read.

Jack's fingers grasped her shoulders gently and forced her to stop, to turn back to him. He saw the tears sliding down over her cheeks. "Kate, what's the matter?" he asked softly.

His tenderness was almost more than she could bear, and induced a fresh onslaught of tears.

Jack didn't want to worry over her, didn't want to care for a crazy woman who thought she was from the past. But the moment he'd untangled himself from LeeAnn and realized Kate was gone, he'd felt a fear he didn't understand and had known he had to find her. "Why'd you leave us like that?"

She shook her head, unable to answer, the emotion caught in her throat.

Jack pulled her to him, crushing her to his chest. "What's wrong, Kate? Tell me. What is it?"

But she wouldn't . . . couldn't answer him, because she only had the truth, and she knew he wouldn't believe that.

TEN

Jack glanced around at the others gathered at the dinner table. Everyone was unusually quiet. He knew Marion and the girls were exhausted, and Liz was doing her best to catch his eye so that she could glare at him for canceling his date with LeeAnn. But it was Kate's quietness that bothered him now, and acknowledging that she could affect him at all just bothered him all the more. He didn't want to acknowledge the feelings that had been simmering within him since the moment he'd laid eyes on her. But denying them, even ignoring them, was beginning to prove impossible.

Ever since he'd found her crying and stumbling down the boardwalk in town that afternoon, she'd seemed withdrawn. She had refused to tell him what was wrong, what had upset her so much. He'd thought maybe it was just him she hadn't wanted to talk to, but now he'd changed his mind. The girls' dinner-table jabber hadn't drawn Kate out, and neither had his mother, whose gift for nonstop gab could usually draw anyone out of her shell. But Kate seemed totally disinclined to talk unless someone specifically directed a question at her.

Worse, she wouldn't even look at Jack.

He speared a piece of barbecued steak from his plate. She was a total enigma, a woman who had been able, without even trying, to penetrate the walls he'd built around his emotions after his wife's death. Jack wanted Kate in his bed, and he wanted her to want him. What he didn't want was to actually care about her. Sending his fork diving into the mound of potatoes in front of him, he glanced at her from beneath half-lowered lids. A sting of anger pierced through him. Whatever was going to happen between them wasn't going to happen until he knew the truth about her, which meant he had to find a way to get her to stop playing this ridiculous charade of being Kate Holliday and level with him.

Somewhere in the back of his mind a little voice whispered, *But are you really sure it's a charade?*

"I'll clear the table," he said suddenly, trying to ignore the games his own mind was starting to play with him. Of course he was sure it was a charade. What else was he supposed to think? That she really was Doc Holliday's mistress, Big-nosed Kate?

No. It was either a charade or she was running from the law, an expert con artist, some weirdo trying to win media attention, or totally crazy. None of those alternatives sounded inviting, yet Jack knew that one of them was probably true.

Marion Ringo smiled at Jack. "Thank you, dear. I think I'll take you up on that offer and go take a nice long, hot bath and retire early." She rose and left the table.

"Me too," Liz said, disappearing before Jack could object.

"I've got some reading to do," Tiffany announced, pushing her chair back and jumping to her feet.

"So do I, Dad," Jessi chirped.

Jack looked at KaraLynn, who was half-asleep in her chair. He reached over and touched her cheek. The child's eyes opened slowly. "Go to bed, pumpkin," he said softly. "You've had a big day. I'll come tuck you in later."

She slid from her chair. "G'night, Daddy," she mumbled, rubbing her eyes as she shuffled toward her room.

Kate knew she should offer to help Jack clear the table and wash the dishes, but that would mean being alone with him—and she didn't feel capable of handling that at the moment.

As if he'd heard her thoughts, sensed her uneasiness, Jack turned to her. "I can do it," he said. "Good night."

She didn't argue. Since the moment he'd pulled her into his arms and tried to comfort her while she'd bawled her eyes out, Kate had known she'd begun to feel things toward Jack Ringo that she had no business feeling. It was too dangerous, could prove much too painful for both of them. They were literally from different worlds, and she could be yanked from his any minute.

Her gaze caressed his face briefly before she dropped her napkin onto the table and rose. Unlike the Ringo she'd known, Jack was a respectable man. An honest man. And she was a gambler, a saloon hostess, and evidently, from what she'd read in the bookstore, would always be known as Doc Holliday's mistress, whether she stayed in this time or went back to her own. But even worse, the book had referred to her as a whore. Pain and anger sliced through her at remembering that. Kate turned toward the door. "Good night," she said softly, thankful the tear that slipped from the corner of her eye had waited until she'd turned her back to Jack Ringo.

Jack watched her walk down the hall. He didn't know what it was about her that drew him, that had his emotions tangled into such a frazzled knot that he could barely think of anything else but her. He only knew that it was tearing him apart inside. He wanted to know the truth about Kate, yet he was afraid. When it came right down to it, he was afraid that the truth might be something he didn't really want to hear. As a man he wanted her to stay, wanted her in his bed, naked and loving, but as a father he needed to protect his family and should force her to leave, no matter what his mother said, or what his own desires tried to demand.

What did they actually know about her? he asked himself. Nothing. If it concerned only him, her evasiveness wouldn't have mattered. But he had his mother, sister, and daughters to consider. They'd befriended Kate immediately, as they did most people. They'd accepted her. Trusted her. Maybe his military training had taken his ability to innocently trust others away from him. Then again, maybe he'd never really had that ability. He couldn't totally accept and trust Kate until he knew the truth about her. Yet deep down inside, the prospect frightened him. He feared the truth might just prove to be the biggest reason of all not to trust her.

"Damned if you do, and damned if you don't," he muttered while clearing off the dinner table. An hour later, with the dishwasher loaded and humming, Jack turned off the lights and walked out onto the moonlit gallery.

Kate was sitting in the porch swing just outside the family-room doors, with Boozer at her feet.

Jack felt a sense of betrayal at seeing his dog there. "I didn't mean to disturb you," he said when Kate looked up at him.

"You're not."

"Want some company?"

She knew she should say no, say go away, Jack Ringo, it's too dangerous, this thing between us. Instead she nodded, because she knew no matter how sensible the reasons were to send him away, she didn't want him to leave.

He sat down beside her. "Beautiful night."

"Yes."

"There was a woman in the saloon today who said she thought she knew you from somewhere."

Kate turned and looked at him sharply. He was lying. There couldn't be anyone in this time who knew her. He was testing her again, as he'd already done several times that day.

Jack smiled. "But I told her that was impossible, 'cause you aren't from around here."

Kate remained still and wary.

He frowned. "So, I guess you didn't know Johnny's wife."

"I didn't know he had one," Kate said.

Jack shrugged. "Most people didn't, so I understand. She lived over by Yuma and was pregnant when he was killed."

"I'm sorry."

He turned to her then. "Why? It wasn't your fault."

Kate stared into the darkness. If she'd known Johnny had been married, she'd never have flirted with him, never even have thought of . . .

"So, what really did happen at the O.K. Corral?" Jack said, throwing the question out as if it was the most innocent one in the world. "Who fired first?"

It took her a moment to escape her thoughts and regrets of the past. When she finally did, she realized instantly that he was still testing her, baiting her. "I don't know," she said coolly. "That happened after I left town."

Jack chuckled. "What's the matter, Kate? Didn't you research that part of Tombstone history?"

She turned to look at him, too angry now to bother keeping her voice low. "I told you, that was after I left town."

He shrugged, ignoring her temper. If he goaded her enough, maybe she'd get tired of the game, tired of these nonsensical lies, and tell him the truth. Again he wondered if she was a woman in trouble. It would explain everything. But if that was it, he couldn't help her if she wouldn't let him. "You know, Kate, I wouldn't have thought a woman as beautiful as you would leave a booming town like Tombstone. I mean, with all the money flowing through it back then, and all the men around, why didn't you just go to work at the Birdcage?"

Her eyes narrowed as her temper flared hotter. "For one thing," she retorted, her tone edged with ice, "I am not . . . I wasn't a whore."

"But you could have served drinks."

"And for another," she continued, "the Birdcage didn't exist when I left, which I'm sure you already knew."

"There were other saloons."

"I wanted to leave."

He jerked around in his seat and stared at her. "Why?"

She hesitated, then walked to the edge of the gallery and stared out into the blackness. For what had to be the thousandth time, she wondered why this had happened to her, and what was going to happen next.

The entire situation frightened her.

"Why?" he demanded again, coming up behind her. Her fragrance filled his senses, the need to touch her burned his fingers, while the yearning to drag her into his arms was almost overwhelming. But Jack resisted. He needed the truth from her first. Needed to know he could trust her with his family, and though he damned himself for it, he needed to know that he could trust her with his feelings before they overpowered him, caused him to do something he wasn't yet ready to do, and made him more vulnerable to her than he wanted to be.

Yet even as the thought flitted through his mind, he knew it was already too late.

"Because I didn't love Doc anymore," Kate said finally, her voice soft and low, almost as if she were speaking only to herself. "Because I knew if I stayed, he'd . . ." She paused, and a long sigh slipped from her lips as she thought about what Doc would most likely have done if she'd stayed in Tombstone.

"He'd what?" Jack urged, his tone hard and demanding. "He'd what, Kate?"

She turned and looked up at him. Tears glistened in her eyes, turned silver in the moonlight. "He'd kill Ringo."

Frustration and fury filled Jack, but he didn't let it show. Instead he smiled and clapped. "Hey, that's good, Kate. Real good. Maybe the ladies' group should use that in the play they're thinking of putting on later this year. And since you know your part so well, you should stick around and be in the thing, maybe you could even help direct it, seeing as you're such an authority and all."

Kate moved quickly, her reaction swift, his slow. The impact of her hand against his cheek stopped Jack's laughter, the sound of flesh slamming against flesh like a crack of lightning in the desert silence.

Jack grabbed her wrist as she spun away from him. "Okay, you've had your fun, Kate. Now just tell me the truth," he said in a whisper that was both scorched fury and pleading entreaty. "Just tell me the damned truth about who you are, and why you're playing these games with me and my family."

Kate jerked her arm free and glared at him. "I've told you the truth," she spat out, then spun around and ran toward the open door of her bedroom.

For several long seconds Jack stood in the darkness alone, staring out at the moon-touched desert. Every ounce of good sense he possessed screamed at him to run as fast and far away from Kate Holliday, or whoever she was, as he could. She was trouble. No matter what the reason for her crazy behavior and claims, he knew she was trouble.

But, at the moment, Jack wasn't concerned about trouble, and he wasn't interested in good sense.

The woman had invaded his life and turned it upside down. She'd seized hold of his emotions, twisted them into a knot, and made him feel things he hadn't even been certain, since Cathy's death, he was capable of feeling again. Kate was a dream and a nightmare combined, and a temptation he was feeling powerless to resist. Without thinking about his actions, without concerning himself about their dangers or potential consequences, Jack crossed the gallery and stormed into her room.

Kate spun around at the sound.

"I want to know the truth, Kate," he said, not stopping until he was in front of her, only the smallest space separating them. "And I want to know it now." He fired off his questions in rapid succession. "Who are you? Why are you here? What do you want?"

Kate struggled to maintain a hold on her own temper. The man was infuriating, and the only reason she didn't lash out at him again was that she knew, had finally admitted to herself, that if the tables were turned, she wouldn't believe her story either. Yet what else could she say? "I told you the truth," she said calmly. "You chose not to believe it." And he never would, she knew now. No matter what she said to Jack Ringo, what had happened to her was something he was never going to believe.

"Then make me believe you," he said. His gaze bored into hers, blue penetrating blue, delving past the tears in her eyes, past the hurt and anger he saw there . . . searching . . . probing.

Kate shook her head, trying to break the spell developing between them, realizing its dangers, its irresistible draw. "I can't. I . . ." Her shoulders sagged and she felt suddenly exhausted. "I don't know how."

With her words, and the sense of defeat that seemed to have settled over her, rational thought, caution, and apprehension slipped from Jack's mind like so much smoke in the wind. Emotion overrode logic, desire conquered wisdom, and the yearnings that had simmered within him for the past two days vanquished all good sense. His hands reached out for her, circled her waist, and drew her to him.

Kate knew she should resist, and knew she couldn't, and Jack took advantage of that fact. Like predator to prey, his lips captured hers, assaulting her already chaotic emotions, conquering her ability to think, inciting the passion she had been fighting desperately to control, to deny, or at least to ignore. His arms drew her against him so tightly that she was molded to his long length, while his mouth worked a gentle torture upon hers that taunted her senses.

Kate felt the fires he had ignited within her merely by his nearness suddenly erupt. Explosion after explosion of want and need swept through her blood with devastating force, turning her hot with desire and exposing a craving in her that was so strong, so raw, she knew she could no longer deny it.

She knew his kiss was sparked by hunger, by lust. She had seen it in his eyes, felt it in his embrace. But she had also seen more, and that both stoked her own desire and frightened her. Now, however, she had no time, energy, or even wish, to evaluate what she had seen.

His mouth was hard and hot on hers, his kiss demanding, almost savage, yet there had been a shadow of loneliness in his eyes that also haunted his embrace, a need to be held, a need to be loved. Even through the haze of her own overwhelming passion, Kate felt that part of Jack that he kept hidden. It emanated toward her now, reached out and beckoned to her like a tangible force. And like a beam of moonlight drawn toward earth, with no ability to change paths or resist the pull, she was drawn to him.

Suddenly nothing else mattered to Kate. Not the differences between them, not the conflict of lies and truths, not even the danger of falling in love with him and then being torn from his world. Only Jack Ringo mattered, only the dark irresistible magic that burned between them, that had touched her heart, her soul, and branded them his forever. She wanted these feelings to burn forever, to sweep them both into eternity, and bind them together for all time.

And even as she yearned for this, a faint, taunting voice deep inside of her kept whispering for her to enjoy him while she could, for tomorrow might not come for her . . . at least in his world.

She kissed him back urgently, desperately. She pressed her body hard to his, moved her arms to draw him even closer, needing to feel his hot, bronzed skin beneath her touch, slide her fingers over every inch of him, so that she could impress the memory of Jack Ringo onto her mind . . . into her soul.

Jack felt her hands skip lightly over his shoulders, her fingers ripple down the hard length of his backbone, hot as flame, gentle as satin, more seductive than anything he'd ever felt. Every cell in his body was aflame with wanting, every inch of him aching to make her his. Wrong or right, truth or lies, he didn't care anymore. He wanted her. That's all he knew, all he cared about.

Her nightgown was a barrier between them he could no longer tolerate. He needed to feel her naked skin pressed against him, feel the sheen of passion that veiled her flesh. He tore his lips away from hers, forced her arms from around him, heard the small moan of despair that escaped her throat at his desertion, and felt his body harden further. Swooping quickly, he slipped his hands under her gown and, rising again, drew it over her head and dropped it to the floor.

For one all-too-brief second his gaze moved over her, appreciating every suddenly revealed naked curve and line. The faint moonlight that flowed into the room through the French doors touched each magnolia-white curve with silver, turned her long hair to a tangle of black silk, and danced amid the tight, dark curls at the apex of her thighs.

Jack felt his breath catch in his throat, felt his longing for her slice through his loins and nearly bring him to his knees. Along with that, for one fleeting moment, fear touched his heart, fear that he couldn't really have her, fear that once he did, he would lose her . . . fear that this woman who had made him feel again, made him start to love again, wasn't even truly real. Then she lifted her arms toward him, and Jack forgot his fear, forgot everything except the fact that Kate was there with him and wanted him as much as he wanted her. He drew her to him, crushing her body against his, and slowly lowered them both onto the bed. His lips pressed a kiss on the crescent-shaped birthmark on the side of her neck, moved to the hollow of her throat, traversed the curve of her shoulder, and finally took her mouth again. The feel of her beneath him, hot and giving, was an intoxicating flame, burning him, seducing him, overwhelming him.

Kate felt his touch everywhere on her body, searing her flesh with each caress, arousing waves of pleasure that volleyed through her relentlessly, continually. His hands were merciless, his fingers touching her in the most erotic ways, in the most sensitive places, robbing her of her last shred of rationality, and leaving her quivering with desire, her body arcing toward his, and silently pleading for more. When he finally entered her, a tearing groan ripped from her lips, and the ravishing continued, until she reveled mindlessly, blissfully, in the hard rhythm of their movements, of their melding together, body and soul.

Long hours later Jack woke to find Kate lying beside him, her finger tracing a small circle on his bare shoulder.

His body instantly began to harden. Yet at the same time doubts and suspicions about her niggled at the back of his mind, as if trying to warn him.

"Johnny had a scar there," Kate said softly, "from a bullet he took from Lyle Bent up in Wichita."

Jack bolted from the bed, his temper flaring. "Still?" he practically bellowed.

Kate frowned, looking up at him in puzzlement.

Then she realized what she'd done. The past. Without thinking, she'd talked about it again.

Not waiting for her to respond, Jack grabbed his pajama bottoms and stalked out of the room, not giving a thought to what time it was, or if anyone else might be up to see him traipsing through the house naked.

ELEVEN

"Oh, Jacky, have you seen—"

Jack stopped just inside the doorway to the kitchen, which was filled with morning sunshine. "Mom," he said, and sighed, "I'm thirty-three years old. Do you think you could just call me Jack?"

Marion stared up at him, frowning, then went on as if he hadn't even spoken. "My brooch? You know, the one your father gave me. I can't seem to find it anywhere."

He walked across the room, grabbed a mug from the counter, and poured himself a cup of coffee. Skirting Thimbles, who was curled up asleep on a rug by the sink and whose fur was now a cloud of lavender-edged white after a half-dozen bathings, Jack moved to stand at the back door. Boozer was lying on the shaded gallery. Jack stared out at the desert, but his eyes weren't seeing the orange, brown, and gold landscape, weren't taking in the mountains in the distance, the tumbleweed at the edge of a knoll several yards away, or the cloudless china-blue sky and brilliantly shining sun that was already heating up the earth and air. Instead, his mind was filled with memories of making love to one of the most intriguing, mesmerizing, and maddening women he'd ever met.

"Jacky, answer me. What's the matter with you?"

"Huh? Oh, sorry, Mom," he mumbled, and tried to banish the image of Kate, naked and passionate, from his mind. "I've . . . got a headache, is all." A headache. He almost snorted. He had a headache all right, and her name was Kate. Or at least that's what she said her name was. Most likely, the way things had been going lately, he'd find her real name under a picture on the FBI's Ten Most Wanted List, tacked up on the wall of the local post office.

"Here," Marion said, handing him a bottle of aspirin. "Get your head out of the clouds and take these." She turned away to caress the African violet sitting on the windowsill, then looked back at Jack. "And have you seen my brooch?"

He frowned. "The cameo?" It was the only one she ever wore. It matched the earrings his father had given her just before he died.

"Yes. I only wear it when I'm dressed up, and as you can see, I am. I'm going into town today for lunch at the church, but I can't find my brooch anywhere." She stroked the plant's leaves and murmured something to it that Jack didn't catch.

"I haven't seen it."

Thimbles sneezed.

"Choo, choo, squawk."

Jack ignored the mimicking of KaraLynn's parrot and looked at Thimbles. The vet had confirmed that the poodle was allergic to the dye Tiffany had used on him and would most likely continue to sneeze until it was totally out of his fur. Jack had suggested shaving him, but his mother had nixed that idea, asking how he'd like to have all his hair shaved off. He looked back at her. "Did you find your earrings, Mom?" he asked, remembering what she'd said the other day.

Boozer came lumbering up to the back door, and Jack pushed the screen open, letting him in. He immediately walked over to Thimbles and lay down.

"My earrings?" She shook her head as if she didn't remember what he was talking about. "Violet needs some vitamins. Her blooms just aren't what they should be, poor dear. Maybe she's pot-bound."

Jack frowned. Was his mother getting . . . He shook the thought away. She'd always been forgetful. Wasn't that why they had a kitchenful of newborn kittens?

"Pretty coincidental, don't you think?" Liz said, breezing into the room.

He turned to stare at his sister. "Coincidental?"

She grabbed a soda from the refrigerator and popped its top. "Yeah. Things start disappearing, and we have a stranger in the house."

Marion gasped. "Elizabeth Ann Ringo, that's a horrible thing to say. Kate would never steal anything."

"Maybe." Liz raised her eyebrows and looked pointedly at Jack. "But you have to admit, Mom, it's pretty coincidental. First Jessi's necklace. Then your earrings. And now your brooch. And all within a couple of days, just when we have a 'guest' in the house."

Jack stared back at her, wanting to agree with his mother and at the same time realizing that Liz could be right. After all, what did they really know about Kate Holliday . . . or whatever her name was?

"Good morning."

They turned toward the doorway.

Jack glimpsed the arrogant smile that tugged at Liz's lips as he turned toward Kate. How long had she been standing in the hall? Long enough to have over-heard Liz accuse her of being a thief?

"Oh, good morning, dear," Marion said brightly, retrieving a cup from the cupboard. "Come and have some coffee. And there's cinnamon rolls on the table, along with a bowl of hard-boiled eggs." She pushed "Violet" to a new spot on the windowsill. "I was just about to leave, but Jack and Liz haven't eaten yet." She started to go, then paused, frowning. "You haven't seen my cameo brooch anywhere, have you, dear? I seem to have misplaced it and Liz thought—"

"My robe looks pretty good on you, Kate," Liz said, cutting her mother off.

Jack watched the interaction between Kate and his sister with both interest and apprehension.

Kate smiled warmly at Marion and Liz, but when she glanced at Jack, a definite frost tinged the air be-tween them. She turned away and moved toward the coffeepot. "I haven't seen a brooch, Marion," she said while pouring herself a cup of coffee, "but I'd be happy to help you look for it."

"There, see, Liz," Marion said indignantly, "I told you—"

"Yes, Mom," Liz said quickly, "you did. Now, why don't you go finish getting yourself ready for that brunch."

"Oh, Violet is still getting too much sun in that spot," Marion said. "I've got to find another place for her, where she'll stay warm."

Liz steered her mother toward the hallway. "I'll fix her, Mom."

Jack ignored his sister and mother, his attention riveted on Kate. He felt an intense, almost painful onslaught of desire start to turn his blood hot and his body hard. His gaze followed her across the room, watching the way the long, lavender velour-and-lace robe subtly draped, but did not hide, the curves his hands had explored so intimately, and swayed gently about the body that had responded with such wanton passion to his lovemaking.

Kate dropped a cube of sugar into her coffee just as KaraLynn skipped into the kitchen.

"Hi, Daddy, hi, Kate." She pulled open one of the doors of the white box Kate had learned was called a refrigerator, and stood on tiptoe to reach a jug of orange juice.

"Here, honey," Kate said, "let me." She grabbed the jug and, retrieving a glass from the cupboard, poured KaraLynn's juice.

Jack watched the easy rapport between Kate and his youngest daughter as KaraLynn drank her juice and Kate tidied the long braid that hung down the child's back.

"There you go," Kate said, tickling KaraLynn's ribs. "Prettiest girl in town."

KaraLynn giggled, drew back, and stood on tiptoe to place her empty glass on the counter. As she released it the glass started to tumble into the sink. Kate caught it.

"Daddy," KaraLynn said, blissfully unaware of the near accident. She bent down and petted Thimbles and Boozer, then stood and looked at Jack. "Can I go over to Robby's house after school today? He has a new puppy and I want to see it."

Jack nodded begrudgingly, because he knew the moment KaraLynn saw the puppy, she wouldn't give him or anyone else in the house a moment's peace until she had one too.

"Go ahead," he said. "Ride the bus home with Robby, but make sure Grandma knows you're going there so she won't call the police when you don't come home from school."

" 'Kay." She skipped out of the room.

"I'll pick you up on my way home," he called after her. KaraLynn was having a small problem with numbers, so he'd enrolled her in a summer-school program in the hope she could catch up with the rest of her class.

" 'Kay," she yelled back.

Kate picked up her coffee cup and started to leave the room. At the door she paused and looked back at Jack. "Ben told me you like to open the Oriental by ten during the festival. I'll be ready to go in half an hour."

Jack glanced at the clock on the wall over the stove. It was only a little after eight. "There's plenty of time for you to have some breakfast."

She looked back at him, surprised, but her gaze was still edged with frost, and Jack wondered, feeling foolish, why he'd said that. Obviously, if she'd wanted breakfast, she'd have moved toward the table, not the door. And, obviously, after the way he'd abruptly left her the night before, she wasn't feeling all that warmly toward him.

"Thank you, but I don't eat breakfast," Kate said coolly, and left the room.

While she showered and readied herself for her second day of work at the Oriental, Jack busied himself searching the house. He looked in every nook and cranny, behind cupboards, under beds, and even shone a flashlight down the sink drains. He found the penknife he'd been looking for the past few months, one of Tiffany's hair clips, several pens, and a couple of quarters. What he didn't find was his mother's brooch, or her earrings, or Jessi's necklace.

Kate entered the living room and paused at seeing Jack on his knees peering under the sofa.

He sensed rather than heard her presence and looked up, then rose to his feet. "Ready?" he asked, feeling like a fool the minute he asked. She was obviously ready, dressed in the costume Liz had worn for the festival last year, a red satin saloon girl's dress that made her look wickedly delicious. His gaze moved over Kate hungrily, in spite of the fact that he'd told himself repeatedly that what had happened between them the night before . . . what he had initiated between them the night before, wasn't going to happen again. A few unspeakable curses zipped through his mind. What had happened between them shouldn't have happened in the first place. He had his family to think of, his girls. He would just have to keep the fiery lust that Kate seemed able to ignite in him under control.

But with her standing there in that dress, it was all he could do not to drag her into his arms, carrying her back to the bedroom and making love to her again. The flared skirt was slit up one side to reveal a very delectable thigh, while the tightly cinched waist accentuated the curve of her breasts, and the low-cut neckline revealed just a hint of cleavage and bared ivory shoulders to his hungry gaze.

With her hair flowing down over one shoulder in a cascade of curls, and a hint of makeup on her face, she was the most beautiful woman Jack had ever seen, and he wanted her with a hunger that was almost agony.

He felt pretty certain that if he looked down, he'd see a bulge in his pants that shouldn't be there. Lacing his fingers together in front of him, he flopped down on the sofa, then crossed one leg on the opposite knee, hopeful of further hiding his problem from her view. "I, uh, I'm waiting for someone to call me back, so, ah, it'll be a few minutes before we can leave. You can, ah, go and have yourself another cup of coffee if you like. And a cinnamon roll."

Kate smiled smugly and, without a word, turned to walk down the hall toward the kitchen.

TWELVE

Two hours later Jack worked beside Ben in the Oriental, popping soda-can tops, pouring drinks, refilling pretzel baskets, and washing glasses. He tried not to think about Kate, or Liz's not-so-subtle accusation, but with Kate waitressing in the saloon, trying not to think about her or be aware of her was just about impossible. Every time he looked up, his gaze invariably zeroed in on her, no matter where she was. He tried to tell himself it was because of the brilliant and provocative red satin dress. But whenever she came near the bar, the scent of jasmine, which he had smelled in her hair the night before as they'd made love, seemed to float across the still air to assail his senses, stoke his memories, and make him want her all the more.

Jack cursed silently. The woman intrigued him, and much as he wanted to, he couldn't deny it. He tried to ignore her, tried to be aloof. The problem was, it didn't work. Each time she came to the bar to place an order, returned to pick it up, walked past him, caught his eye, desire twisted in his loins like a tormenting snake.

Before he'd settled down and married Cathy, Jack had been a real ladies' man. Love 'em and leave 'em, that had been him. He'd never had a problem getting a woman into his bed, or walking away from her later. Until Cathy. She'd stolen his heart and made him want to settle down.

He watched Kate serve a trayful of sodas to a family seated at a table near the door. A sigh of frustration slipped from his lips. He wasn't in love with her, that he knew for certain. All he had to do was remember how he'd felt about his late wife, the sweet, easy, comfortable love they'd shared, and he knew it wasn't love he felt for Kate. No, what he felt for her was hot, burning, gut-gnawing passion. His mind was frustrated because she wouldn't tell him the truth about who she was, and his body was frustrated because it seemed to be in a constant state of desire. He didn't love her, but he sure as hell still wanted her.

And now, to make matters worse, Liz's accusation was haunting him, making him feel like a two-bit louse for giving it even an inkling's worth of credence.

"Sure does spark up the place, doesn't she?" Ben remarked, glancing at Jack.

He didn't answer. He'd had enough goading and innuendo from Ben in the past two hours regarding Kate to last him a lifetime. Jack glanced at his watch and grabbed the holster and gun from a wooden hook behind the bar. "Just about time for the showdown," he said, strapping the holster around his hips, then shifting it around until it settled into place.

"Got a pretty good crowd out there waiting on you," Ben said, smiling. "Who wins today, Johnny or the gambler?"

Jack grabbed his Stetson. "Who do you think?" he said, and chuckled for the first time that morning.

Kate heard the soft rumble of Jack's laugh and turned from the table of ladies she had been talking to. Her heart did a funny little flip as she looked toward the bar, expecting to see Jack, and instead saw Johnny.

Her breath caught in her throat. It had happened. Without Indians, a stagecoach crash, or even a bed of cactus, it had happened. Tears instantly filled her eyes. She hurriedly wiped them away with trembling fingers and blinked.

"Change my order to lemonade, would you, honey?" one of the ladies said to her. "I don't think I can handle any carbonation this afternoon."

Kate jerked around and stared down at the woman, shocked to see her still seated at the gaming table, her head of ridiculous blonde curls popping out from beneath a silly-looking hat that KaraLynn had explained to Kate the night before was called a baseball cap, and a caricature of a mouse wearing gloves imprinted on the front of her shirt. Relief flowed through Kate. She looked back at the bar. It wasn't Johnny, but Jack whom she'd seen, and it wasn't the first time she'd made that mistake.

Kate's body felt suddenly weak as she stared at Jack. Sunlight flowed through the front window of the saloon and cast him in brilliant light and veiled shadow, accentuating the broadness of his shoulders and the muscular curves of his arms, while darkening the chestnut strands that touched the collar at his nape, and leaving those one-of-a-kind blue eyes obscured beneath the brim of his hat.

Kate shivered at the resemblance and the memories it conjured up in her mind.

One of the conchas on the hatband of Jack's Stetson caught the sunlight and reflected toward Kate's eye in a burst of dazzling silver. She watched as he drew the gun that lay settled against his right thigh from its holster and spun its cylinder to make certain it was loaded, then repeated the process with his other gun.

Suddenly a blur of white moved across her line of vision and Kate unconsciously stiffened.

"Jack."

He nearly groaned at recognizing LeeAnn's voice, but there was no escape. Looking up, he saw her lazing against the bar across from him, leaning forward to give him what was obviously meant to be a tempting view of her cleavage.

"I've made us a reservation at Nellie's for lunch," she practically purred.

Jack shook his head. "Sorry, LeeAnn, I've got to do the showdown now."

"I know that, I meant after." She smiled slyly and brushed a lace-gloved hand suggestively across the top of one breast.

The look in her eyes reminded Jack of one he'd

seen on Miss Kitty's face when she chased a mouse in the barn. It wasn't one that made him comfortable.

"LeeAnn, I'm really busy with the—"

"You've got to eat, Jack. And, anyway, I've got something I need to talk to you about." Her smile widened. "Please. It's really—" She suddenly stopped and looked down.

Boozer stood beside her, his nose buried in the mound of pristine white lace ruffles that cascaded down the back of her long form-hugging gown.

"Eck, get away before you get drool on me," LeeAnn said, wrinkling her nose and shooing at the dog.

"He doesn't drool," Jack said flatly.

LeeAnn smiled. "Jack, it's important." Her smile disappeared and she frowned as if something was troubling her. "I need your advice."

He nodded, purposely not looking at either Ben or Kate. "Okay. I'll meet you there." He'd try once more to convince her that he wasn't looking for a wife, he said to himself.

LeeAnn's smile returned, smug and satisfied. "Good." She glanced in the mirror over the bar and caught sight of Kate. "And don't stand me up again, Jack," she purred softly, "or this time I just might not forgive you so easily." She leaned over even farther and blew Jack a kiss. He forced himself to smile at the gesture, at the same time afraid she was going to pop right out of her bodice. "I'll meet you at Nellie's," he said, and strode around the bar. Out of the corner of his eye he caught sight of Kate standing near one of the tall windows that faced Fifth Street. He knew she was watching him, had been watching him converse with LeeAnn, and told himself he didn't care. It didn't matter. Jack walked around the bar. It was time for the shoot-out.

He didn't want to look at Kate, and with each step he took toward the swinging doors that led to the street, he told himself not to look at her. He needed to concentrate on the showdown, give the people who'd come to Tombstone for the festival their money's worth. But one look into Kate's eyes made him momentarily forget everything but her.

She stared at him, her gaze moving to the holsters slung low upon his hips, and the two guns that he'd slid into them. For just a moment, as she stared at the curved wooden handles and the notches carved into them, she felt fear seize her heart and chill her to the bone.

Then a young boy darted into the saloon, laughing loudly and jabbing a toy gun at another child who followed him. Reality pressed itself back upon Kate. She nearly sagged with relief. Whoever was waiting outside in the street to face Jack in a walk-down, it was all right. There was no chance that Jack was going to die, no chance he would never walk back through those doors, no chance she would never see his smile again, feel the crush of his lips, or the length of his body pressed against her own.

The last thought that flitted through her mind surprised her, especially since it had managed to slip through both the anger she'd felt since his abrupt departure from her bed the night before, and the hurt that had followed. She didn't want to care about Jack Ringo, but it was too late for that.

Jack might have come to her bed last night, but that had merely been to fulfill his needs as a man. The person he really cared about was obviously LeeAnn Clay.

Kate gave an exaggerated swish of her skirt, turned her back to Jack, and stared out the window at the empty side street. She was probably only attracted to him because he reminded her of Johnny. They looked so much alike, even their mannerisms were similar.

Just then Boozer rubbed his lanky body against Kate's leg. She reached down and patted the dog's head.

"Good luck, Jack, honey," LeeAnn said in a sultry voice as he pushed open the saloon's batwing doors.

Kate glanced over her shoulder and saw LeeAnn slide a hand possessively up the length of Jack's arm, then stand on tiptoe and tilt her head up to press her lips to his cheek.

Jack jumped slightly, not having been aware she'd approached. The woman was like a damned cat, he swore to himself silently, and considering some of the cats he'd come into contact with over the years, that wasn't necessarily a compliment. He tore his gaze away from Kate and nodded to LeeAnn. "Thanks," he grumbled.

"Hey, Ringo," a voice from outside yelled, "come on out and meet your Maker."

Jack settled a smug, sneering smile on his face and walked outside to the cheer of the tourists crowding the boardwalks.

❖━━━❖

Jack stared at LeeAnn, unable to believe what she'd just asked him. "That's what was so important?" he finally said, wincing and lowering his voice as he saw several people turn to look at him. "You want me to help you decide what kind of new car to buy?"

Her red Corvette was only a year old, and the flashiest in town, if you didn't count Mrs. Two Horse's pink '57 Cadillac convertible, with the raccoon tail flying from the radio antenna, six-gun door handles, and four-foot-wide steer horns mounted on its hood.

LeeAnn nodded, a serious look on her face, unaware of the anger Jack was struggling to hold back. "Yes. Daddy . . ." She paused, flipped her long blonde hair over her shoulder, and started again. "My father wants me to take over the breeding program on the ranch and says I'll need something a little more rugged to get around in."

Jack stared at her, his disbelief growing. Clay was going to turn his breeding program over to LeeAnn? Wondering if the man was crazy, he asked, "Why?"

LeeAnn shrugged. "He says I need to start learning how the place runs, take on some responsibility."

Jack couldn't argue with that. "So, what do you want from me?"

"I told you." She smiled and reached across the table to run a finger down the length of his hand. "Advice."

He pulled back, slowly, so as not to insult her. "On?"

LeeAnn shrugged. "What to buy, of course."

Under the table Jack felt her foot slide up the side of his leg. "I'm sure your father could help you, Lee-Ann," he said. "He probably has something in mind anyway."

"He just said buy an SUV, whatever that is. And he's flying to New York right after the festival, so he can't help." She smiled. "I thought maybe we could drive up to Tucson tomorrow and look at some cars together."

Jack moved his leg and shook his head. "Can't spare the time, LeeAnn, not with the festival going on."

Her smile suddenly turned pouty. "But, Jack, this is important. I mean, I don't want to get a car you don't like, because, well, if we . . . you know, get together, it'll belong to us, and . . ."

Jack sighed. So that was it. He sat forward and took one of her hands in his. This time he was going to make her understand. "LeeAnn, look, I—"

"Hey, Ringo, whaddaya doin' with my woman?"

Jack nearly groaned aloud. His first inclination was to tell Stan Richards to bug off, but as he glanced over his shoulder toward where the man stood in the doorway, he saw that every eye in the restaurant, as well as a good crowd in the street, was watching him and waiting for "Johnny Ringo" 's reaction. He pushed his chair back and rose slowly to his feet, turning to face Stan at the same time.

"If you can't keep 'em satisfied, Richards . . ." Jack sneered, then smiled and shrugged, letting the implication hang in the air.

Stan instantly went for his gun.

Jack's exploded with sound before Stan even cleared leather. Stan clutched his chest, staggered back out into the street, and fell to the ground.

The crowd cheered, then began to disperse.

Jack turned back to LeeAnn, who was also standing now. "LeeAnn, I—"

She waved a hand at him and set her plumed hat back on her head. "I've got to go meet Daddy now," she said. "Call me tonight and let me know when we can go to Tucson."

Jack was about to tell her they weren't going to Tucson when she slipped her arms around him and pressed her lips to his, right in the middle of Nellie's restaurant. Then she just as quickly pulled away and hurried toward the door. "Call me."

He paid the tab, grabbed his hat, and ramming it onto his head, strode from the restaurant toward the saloon. The black cloud that seemed to hang over his head, and the black mood that had invaded him, did more to transform Jack into the dark semblance of a gunslinger than any costume or playacting showdown could . . . and caused more than a few nearby tourists to hurriedly abandon the boardwalk.

Ben looked up in surprise as Jack smashed through the Oriental's swinging doors. "What's the matter?" he asked as Jack flung the Stetson onto a wall hook. "Lose the showdown?"

"That would have been preferable," Jack snapped. "Than what?"

Jack's gaze quickly roamed the saloon's interior as he unbuckled his holster. "Where's Kate?"

"Took a break."

He looked toward the end of the bar. "Where's Boozer?"

"Went with Kate."

That surprised him. Normally, the big bloodhound never left the bar or the house unless he was with Jack. He reached into a bucket of ice, grabbed a can of soda, popped its top, and took a long drink, hoping to cool off both his body and his temper. It didn't work. At least not on his temper. He slammed the can down onto the bar, ignoring the liquid that shot up through the can's opening, and glared at Ben. "You know what was so damned important? A car," he said, before Ben could respond. "LeeAnn wants me to help her pick out a new car."

Ben chuckled. "Sounds pretty important to me."

"Yeah, I guess so, considering the rattletrap you drive."

"So, did you tell her?"

Jack shook his head, knowing what Ben was referring to. "I was about to, had even started, but Stan Richards came in and called me out."

Ben remained silent.

"Well, dammit, there were too many people watching for me to just tell him to get lost," Jack snapped. "What'd you expect me to do?"

Ben raised his hands as if in surrender and took a step back, fighting to hide a grin. "Hey, I didn't say a word, boss."

"You didn't have to," Jack grumbled.

"Yeah, well, you got another problem anyway."

"Great," Jack said. "What now? My mother burn down the church?"

Ben looked confused.

"Never mind."

"Liz came by while you were gone," Ben said.

"Terrific. What'd she do now?"

"She asked me to open the safe so she could get into that old jewelry box you keep in there. Said she was going to wear Ellie Ringo's ruby earrings to the party they're having over at the Crystal Palace tonight."

"Yeah, so?" Jack didn't see what the problem was.

"Well, ah . . ."

"What!" Jack said with a growl.

"The prize money for the shoot-out contest is gone."

Shock jerked at Jack's body, and his hand clenched the aluminum soda can he was still holding. The last of his soda spurted into the air as the can's sides folded inward. "What do you mean it's gone?" he demanded.

Ben shrugged and motioned for Jack to lower his voice. "I mean," he said pointedly, "it's gone."

THIRTEEN

"Have you called the sheriff?" Jack asked.

"Not yet."

Jack threw the crushed can into a nearby garbage bin with such force that it bounced off the other cans already there and nearly jumped back out at him. He paid no attention. "And why the hell not?"

"Because," Ben said, straining to keep his voice low so that their customers wouldn't hear, "I didn't know if you'd taken it for some reason. Or moved it."

"You know damned well I wouldn't have—" Jack stopped. He was being unreasonable. "Well, call him now."

Ben immediately picked up the phone and dialed the sheriff's number.

Ten minutes later a short man with a barrel chest and silver-white hair peeking out from beneath a cowboy hat walked through the swinging doors of the Oriental and paused to remove the dark glasses resting on the bridge of his Karl Malden–like nose. He spotted Jack behind the bar and walked over to him. "Ben said you got a problem here." He glanced at the several dozen tourists sitting at the saloon's various tables. "Looks peaceful enough."

"It's not that kind of problem." Jack waved Lyle Cunningham toward the rear of the bar, then turned into a hallway and preceded him into the back office. "Someone stole my contest money out of the safe."

The sheriff's white brows soared upward. "Didn't you have the thing locked?"

"Of course it was locked," Jack snapped.

"Then how—"

"I don't know. All I know is that when Ben opened the safe to get something out for my sister a little while ago, the money wasn't there."

"Why didn't you open the safe for your sister?"

"Because I wasn't here," Jack said, seeing instantly where the sheriff's question was heading. "And Ben didn't take it."

Lyle shook his head. "Didn't say he did. Just wondered, was all. Got a new employee, don'tcha?"

Jack stiffened. "Kate doesn't know the combination. She doesn't even know the safe's here."

The sheriff rolled his beefy shoulders in a shrug.

"Lyle, without that money," Jack said, "I can't afford to go through with the shoot-out contest."

The sheriff's heavy brows drew together as a frown crinkled his forehead and his mud-colored eyes took on a more worried look. "Posters all over town, Jack. Be kinda hard to cancel the thing now."

"Be kind of hard to pay the winner too," Jack retorted caustically, "if I don't have the money."

"You keep this room locked when you ain't in it?" Lyle looked at the door, the top half of which was old, bubbled glass. The name Mattie could still be seen painted on the glass in black letters, though they were badly faded. No one knew for sure if that meant the room had once been used by the wife Wyatt Earp had brought with him to Tombstone, then left for Josie Marcus, or if it referred to some other Mattie.

"No," Jack said. "I never really felt the need."

"Hmmph. Too bad." The sheriff stared down at the simple combination dial safe. "With all these tourists in town, coulda been just about anybody stole that money, Jack. And that kinda lock"—he shook his head—"well, it ain't the best you could get, you know."

Jack's heart sank, along with his hopes of ever seeing his prize money again.

"When's the last time you saw the money there?" Lyle asked, breaking into Jack's thoughts.

"Few days ago." He had a feeling he knew exactly what the sheriff's response was going to be.

"Then it could be that it's been missing for a few days."

Jack nodded, while trying to think of something he could sell to raise the prize money. Nothing came to mind. He'd have to call *Aviation Monthly* and see if they were interested in buying the article he'd sent them the previous week.

"Maybe you should get Boozer in here," Lyle said.

"Let him sniff around a bit, see what he comes up with."

"Without giving him something to look for," Jack said angrily, his frustration momentarily overwhelming him, "he'll come up with nothing more than a desire to take a nap or raid my liquor shelf."

The sheriff chuckled. Everyone knew that stumbling into Jack's liquor shelf and licking up everything that spilled was how Boozer had gotten his name.

After a few more minutes of useless discussion, ending with the sheriff saying he'd do what he could, Jack returned to the bar to find the room packed with tourists.

"Kate's back," Ben said over the steady hum of conversation. He nodded toward where she stood beside a table of portly senior citizens, each decked out in flowery summer shirts, straw hats, and sandals.

One of the men said something to Kate, and she laughed, the throaty sound floating across the room to Jack.

He filled several orders and, when there was a lull, told Ben to take a break. Leaning back against the rear of the bar, he watched Kate move easily among the tourists, talking, laughing, and taking orders. But even as the heat of desire niggled at Jack's insides and gave him a restless edge, Liz's words of accusation danced around in his thoughts, and a new suspicion reared its ugly head.

What did they really know about her? It was a question he'd asked himself before, and the answer hadn't changed. All of her claims were ridiculous.

Maybe her name really was Kate Holliday, but she certainly wasn't *the* Kate Holliday, because that would mean she had been born in 1855, and as far as Jack was concerned, she looked a far cry from one hundred and forty-two years old.

But she'd done her research well, he had to give her that. She knew more than the average person did about Doc Holliday, Wyatt Earp, and the way Tombstone had been in the 1880s. And she was a good actress. Now, along with the question of why she was keeping up this charade, another had slipped into his mind to taunt him—was she also a thief? He didn't relish even considering that question, but he knew he'd be a fool not to.

The swinging doors opened, and glancing toward them, Jack saw Liz enter. She walked up to the bar and slapped an envelope onto its surface. "You can put the earrings back into the safe for me," she said, fire flashing from her eyes. "I won't need them tonight after all."

His brows rose questioningly as he set a can of soda before her. "What happened?"

"Ken and I had an argument," she snapped, referring to the local rancher she'd been dating for the past several months. "He doesn't want to go to the party at the Palace. He wants to go up to Tucson."

"So, go to the party without him."

"Oh, right, wouldn't that look great."

"It would look," Jack said, leaning his arms onto the bar, "like you wanted to go to the party."

"Will you come with me?"

He shook his head. "Sorry, sis, my hot-and-heavy partying days are over."

"Oh yeah, I forgot," she teased, "you're an old man now with a family."

Jack laughed. "That's me. The old curmudgeon."

"Except you need a Mrs. Curmudgeon."

Jack's smile instantly disappeared as the old hurt cut through him. It wasn't searing anymore, not like it had been, and Jack was thankful for that, but it was still there, and he knew it would be for a long time. If he'd gone to Tucson with Cathy that day as she'd wanted him to, maybe he'd have been driving, and she wouldn't be dead. "I had one. Remember?" He turned away and began putting dirty glasses into a dishwasher beneath the bar.

Liz turned around and, with her elbow propped on the bar, looked at Kate. "How's she doing?" she asked over her shoulder. "Any tourists claiming their purses were snatched or pockets picked?"

Jack remained silent. He wasn't about to tell Liz that the prize money for the shoot-out was missing. Liz wanted him to marry LeeAnn, and instead of believing that he wasn't in love with her best friend, she'd obviously decided that Kate was the obstacle preventing their union. The first thing Liz would say was that Kate had stolen the prize money.

But even though he didn't want to hear Liz say it, Jack couldn't deny the suspicions that lurked in his own mind. All he could do was try to ignore them, as well as ignore the damned heat of desire that was eating him up inside. The trouble was, all he had to do was think about Kate, or merely look at her, and suspicion and desire assaulted him like a bullet between the eyes— hot, instant, and all-consuming. And maybe even deadly.

About an hour before closing time, Marion walked into the Oriental.

"Mom," Jack said, surprised. "What are you doing here?"

"Oh, I had to come back to pick up a few things. Jessi and Tiffany are in the car, but as long as I was back in town, I thought I'd stop in for a bottle of wine to go with dinner. We're having chicken."

He nodded, grabbed one of his better whites from beneath the bar, and handed it to her. "I might be a little late," he said. "I let Ben go early today, and I've got to tally up the day's receipts. And would you mind picking KaraLynn up at Robby's for me?" He glanced at Kate, who was sitting alone at a table near the window. "Things are pretty slow now, most of the tourists have gone for the day. Why don't you take Kate home with you? She's probably tired."

Jack wasn't about to tell his mother, or anyone else, the real reason he wanted to be alone in the saloon.

"Oh Jacky," Marion wailed suddenly, "you haven't been taking care of Scruffy and Benjamin."

Jack looked at his mother in total confusion, until he remembered that those were the names of the tall cactus and delicate-leaved ficus she'd brought into the saloon the week before. "Sorry, Mom, I guess I—"

"Neglected them, that's what you've done," she said, while examining the ficus's leaves. "Oh dear." She shook her head. "You obviously haven't even bothered to water poor Benjamin, and you moved Scruffy out of the sun." She glared at Jack. "They're not happy with you, Jacky."

"Of course not," Jack mumbled, "I'm a plant abuser, destined for prison." He looked up quickly to make certain his mother hadn't heard him. He knew if she did, he was in for one very long, very heated lecture on how plants were just as alive and feeling as he was.

He smiled as his last customer left, then walked around the bar to his mother. "Mom"—he put an arm around her shoulders and steered her toward the door—"I'll take care of them, I promise."

"You'll put—"

"I'll move Scruffy in front of the window so he gets more sun, and I'll give Benjamin a whole pitcherful of water."

She looked up at him warily. "All right, but don't you forget, Jacky."

At the door he stopped and looked back at Kate, finding that she'd been watching the exchange between him and his mother. "I've got a little bookkeeping to do after we close," he said, "and it looks like the streets are just about empty. Why don't you go ahead home with my mother."

Kate nodded and stood. "Thanks. I am kind of tired."

Five minutes after they left, Jack hung the "Closed" sign in the window, locked the front doors, took the cash register till from beneath the bar, and carried it into his office. He sat down with a sigh, not wanting to think about why he couldn't leave the day's receipts for morning, but he was unable to help himself. Only three people had access to the till: himself, Ben, and Kate. He'd trust Ben with his life, so if the receipts didn't tally, that could only mean . . . well, he didn't want to think about what that would mean.

An hour later, after going over the figures twice, he finally allowed himself to believe he hadn't made a mistake and sighed in relief. At least *this* wasn't a problem.

The moment Jack walked into the house, he was assailed by the sound of laughter. A smile crept onto his face. The girls were probably watching their favorite old reruns. He walked into the family room and stopped, surprised. The television wasn't even on. Instead, Tiffany, Jessi, and KaraLynn were sitting on the floor with Kate, all hovering over a Monopoly board.

"Hey, Dad," Tiffany said, looking up at him. "We're teaching Kate how to play Monopoly."

He leaned against the armoire-type entertainment center, arms crossed over his chest. "You mean there's actually someone in the world who doesn't know how to play?" he asked, looking at Kate.

She looked back but didn't smile.

"Yeah," KaraLynn piped up, "Kate. She's my partner, and we're beating Jessi and Tiff."

"Are not," Jessi said. "I own three hotels, and you

guys only own one. And we have two Get Out of Jail Free cards too."

"Yeah," KaraLynn said, "but me and Kate own Boardwalk and the train places and the water faucet and"—she looked down and counted quickly—"eight houses and lotsa money."

Jessi rolled the dice, and the others, including Kate, immediately seemed to forget about Jack.

"Pay us, pay us." KaraLynn squealed with delight as Tiffany moved her piece and landed on Boardwalk.

Jack watched them for several more minutes, then settled down on the sofa, not quite sure how he felt about his girls' ready acceptance of Kate. Was this his mother's influence? Or an indication that his wariness and suspicions about this woman—who had so unceremoniously dropped into their lives and made him feel things he wasn't sure he really wanted to feel again—were so far off base as to be ludicrous?

Kate seemed genuinely to care for Tiffany, Jessi, and KaraLynn, and was obviously comfortable with them. But somehow that fact made Jack feel anything but easy about the situation. He knew she was hiding something. Did she have children of her own? Had she lost a child? Was she on the run from an abusive husband, or someone else? The questions zipped through his mind until he wanted to slam a fist down on the arm of the sofa, drag her up to him, and demand she confide in him, tell him the truth.

❖———————❖

Jack walked across his bedroom, threw open the French doors, and stepped out onto the gallery. Dinner was over, the table had been cleared, his mother and Liz were watching television in the family room, and the girls were in their rooms.

The sun had disappeared behind the ragged peaks of the mountains about half an hour before, but streaks of orange and gold and blue still slashed across the sky, as if resisting the blackness slowly descending on them.

But Jack hadn't come outside to appreciate the landscape, or even get a breath of fresh air. He'd come in search of Kate.

FOURTEEN

"Thinking about old friends?" Jack asked, spying Kate sitting on the porch swing. He didn't know why he'd said that. It was antagonistic, and the last thing he felt like doing was antagonizing her.

He was surprised to see Boozer beside the swing, snoring softly and contentedly as Kate's fingers lightly traced a circle through the thick short hairs on his back.

She glanced up at Jack. Moonlight danced within the long waves of her dark hair, but he was uncertain whether the fire he saw in her blue eyes was a spark of anger or merely a reflection.

Kate smiled, and Jack felt flushed with relief.

"As a matter of fact," she answered softly, "I was." She had made a decision that afternoon, after seeing him with LeeAnn Clay. Maybe she'd been sent here by fate, the heavens, or whatever, to be with Jack. And then again, maybe she hadn't. Maybe it had merely been some kind of accident. She didn't know. What she did know was that she couldn't continue to hide her identity. At least not from him. He might not want to accept it, might not want to believe it, but she wouldn't continue to hide it. Even if it made him angry.

"Sorry I blew up at you like that last night." Jack smiled. "Can I sit down?"

She nodded, and he joined her on the swing. An aching need and a thousand pinpricks of heat invaded her body the moment he sat and his body touched hers. No man had ever affected her the way Jack Ringo did, and she had a feeling, both sinking and elated, that no man ever would.

"I've been thinking."

Kate didn't look at him but continued to stare out at the desert.

"And wanting to talk to you," Jack went on. "There's something between us." He chuckled self-consciously. "I guess that's obvious."

"Yes," she whispered.

He turned in his seat so that he was almost facing her. "I don't know where it's going to lead, Kate, but . . ." Jack paused for a long moment, and Kate thought he wasn't going to say anything more.

She opened her mouth to speak, to tell him that it couldn't go anywhere, that it was impossible for her to offer him any more than the moment, if that, but he continued before she had a chance.

"I have to know the truth about you, Kate. I have to know who you are."

"You won't believe me."

"I'll try."

Kate nodded. He was asking for the truth. She'd decided not to skirt around it just to keep from angering him. There was no reason not to answer him—except that she feared that once she did, he would turn away from her again.

"My name is Kate Holliday," she said, still refusing to look at him. "A lot of people knew me as Big-nosed Kate, and Doc Holliday's wife, though I never really was. Not legally anyway. Unless you consider it common-law."

"Kate," Jack said, unable to keep the frustration from his tone.

She turned and held his gaze, determined this time to finish. "You said you'd try."

He nodded. "Okay."

"I met Doc in Wichita. He didn't hide the fact that he was sick, and I didn't care. There was something between us right from the start."

"Oh, hell." Jack bolted from his seat and stormed toward his room. "I can't listen to this."

Kate sat on the swing for several long minutes, silently mulling over her own thoughts, then she rose and followed him.

He was standing near his bureau, staring at a framed picture of his great-great-great-grandfather.

"I fell in love with Doc," Kate said, pausing to stand behind Jack. "But he was a hard man to love. Doc was dying, so tenderness wasn't easy for him to accept, or give."

Jack turned to look at her.

"Wyatt was Doc's best friend," she continued, expecting him at any moment to explode or walk out on her again, "and in spite of the fact that the rest of the Earps didn't like Doc, we followed them to Tombstone. But by then Doc and I were fighting more than we were loving."

Memory of what she'd read in the bookstore about Doc's death assailed her and brought feelings of guilt and regret. She should have stayed in Tombstone, gone to Colorado Springs with Doc, to the sanitarium, and held his hand at the end. Tears slid down her cheeks, but Kate was unaware of them until Jack reached out and brushed one away. Without a word of whether he believed her or not, he pulled her into his arms, drawing her body against his, and claimed her lips.

Thoughts of Doc and the past disappeared, but in spite of the desire Jack's touch ignited in her body, the yearning need to give in to it, and to him, Kate forced herself to pull away from him. She tore her lips from the sweet taste of his and pushed a hand against his chest, but Jack's arms around her held tight.

Kate looked up at him, about to tell him this was wrong, that it wasn't fair to him, that he wasn't fair to her—making her fall in love with him when she knew it most likely couldn't last.

"No," he said, his voice guttural, his gaze pained. "Don't deny us now, Kate. I couldn't stand it."

His words cut straight to her heart, and Kate found that whatever willpower she had left wasn't enough to help her turn away from him or deny that she wanted him. Moving her hand to the front of her blouse, she slowly unbuttoned it, released the front hook of her brassiere, then stood still, her body on fire, as Jack, the tension in his body quickly replaced by passion, pushed the straps from her shoulders.

When they were both naked, he drew her back to him, crushing her naked breasts into the coarse chestnut hairs that covered his chest. His mouth ravished hers as his arms held their bodies tightly to each other and he rubbed his arousal against her stomach.

A moan of desire ripped from Kate's throat. Fire was consuming her body, searing her blood. Her arms slid around his neck, and she moved as he moved.

When he pulled his head back and drew away from her, she nearly screamed. Then she felt his lips close over her right breast and his tongue circle her nipple teasingly, while his hands moved over the rest of her body like satin gloves inflicting torturous ecstasy.

Feelings, yearnings she had never before experienced, never known she even possessed, ripped from her soul. She felt as if she were being devoured by need, and his touch was all that could save her.

He pulled her down to the bed, his mouth still clinging to her breast, her fingers slipping through the dark tangles of his hair as the flames of need burned hotter, brighter, and threatened to rob her mind of everything but her desire to be taken by this man.

She felt his hand on her thigh and willingly, eagerly spread her legs apart. His fingers slid through her soft black curls, then sank deep within her.

A pulsing wave of rapture swept her along, and Kate murmured his name over and over, every muscle in her body clenching in tension, in need. "Jack, Jack, I need you now," she said, then gasped. "Please."

He entered her with a force more desperate, more conquering than anything she'd ever felt. Kate cried out as her body tensed at the invited assault.

A shudder of desire ripped through Jack, and he paused and looked down at her.

She stared into his eyes, his passion having turned them as dark as sapphire, and suddenly she knew the truth. In the beginning, only a few short days before, she had wondered, nearly convinced herself, that she was attracted to Jack Ringo only because he reminded her so much of Johnny. Now she knew that wasn't true. Johnny Ringo would never have known how to relate to three little girls. He would never have rocked a child to sleep after she'd had a bad dream, sat on the kitchen floor and helped another name her kittens, or held the hand of a young girl on the verge of womanhood as he gently explained to her why she was still too young for so many things. Johnny never would have had the patience to deal with an older woman's eccentricities, a sister's antagonism, or a strange woman's wild story of traveling through time. And he never would have made love to a woman as selflessly as Jack was making love to her.

"Love me," Kate whispered, her need for Jack Ringo overwhelming her. "Now."

Her words released a floodgate of desire and feelings within Jack. He plunged into Kate as she arched up to meet him. Her cry of satisfaction pushed him beyond control. He drew out and pushed back into her with frenzied force, mindlessly giving in to the hungers that drove him.

She moved desperately against him, pulling him deeper within her, both physically and emotionally. His hands moved over her body, touching everywhere, igniting need and want with every caress, and as the tension in her coiled tighter and tighter, she joyfully returned the favor.

"You're killing me," he ground out between ragged breaths, his lips against her neck.

But whether his words meant he needed her to stop or go on with her assault against his body, Kate didn't know. She knew only that for her, it was too late for either. Only seconds after he'd spoken, an explosion of pleasure erupted within her with such force that she cried out his name and dug her fingers into his shoulders as the fires of her release swept through every cell of her body.

"Kate," Jack said with a groan, and with her name on his lips he shuddered helplessly, spasms of pleasure ripping through him as his seed poured into her body.

Long moments later both lay still, Jack having slid from atop her to lie at her side, one leg still draped over hers, his arms holding her tight.

Lord in heaven, Kate thought, still dazed with passion, she had never experienced anything like what had just happened between them, never felt a man's need so intensely, never given herself up to a man so completely.

His hand moved to her breast and his fingers slowly began a teasing caress of her nipple. As Kate felt the fires of desire begin to stir to life within her again, she smiled. It was going to be a long, and most pleasurable, night. And she would worry about tomorrow . . . tomorrow.

Several hours later Jack jerked awake, not certain what it was that had pulled him so rudely from his sleep. He lay still on the bed, his arms wrapped around Kate, and stared up into the darkness.

A sense of satisfaction filled him as he became fully aware of her lying beside him.

Then the telephone rang again, the shrill sound cutting through the silence.

Jack swore softly and glanced at the lighted numbers of the radio clock on his bureau. It wasn't as late as he'd expected—barely nine. He slipped away from Kate and grabbed the phone just as it began to ring again. "Ringos," he said into the mouthpiece, his tone gruffer than he'd intended.

"Jack?" LeeAnn said. "Is that you?"

He fought down the rancor and frustration that filled him at recognizing LeeAnn's voice. "Yes," he said simply, waiting for her to say why she was calling. He hoped it was to talk to Liz.

"Jack, please . . . you've got to come over."

"LeeAnn, I—"

"Please, Jack," she said, sounding frantic. "Please. It's urgent."

Before he could respond, the line went dead. Jack held the receiver away from his ear and stared at it, trying to decide whether or not to call the sheriff. Her abrupt hang-up filled him with apprehension.

"What's the matter?" Kate asked, trying to stifle the jealousy that had filled her the moment she'd heard him mention LeeAnn Clay's name.

"I don't know." He sat up, swung his legs over the side of the bed, and reached for his jeans.

Kate pushed herself up to a sitting position and, holding the bedsheet to her breast, drew her legs up to her, as if to tuck in the hurt that had suddenly assailed her. "You're leaving?"

"Something's wrong. Hopefully"—he slipped on a T-shirt, then leaned down to brush his lips across hers—"I won't be long. Go back to sleep."

Moments later, as Jack drove away from the house with Boozer riding in the bed of the pickup, Liz let the curtain fall back into place before the living-room window and smiled.

FIFTEEN

It was normally a fifteen-minute drive to the Clay ranch. Jack cut several minutes off his time by taking a back road and speeding, still worried that something was wrong.

He glanced at his cell phone, silently debated whether or not to call the sheriff's office, then jerked the receiver from its cradle and punched out the number.

"Tombstone Sheriff's Office, Maggie Shallene," the night clerk said upon answering.

"Maggie, this is Jack Ringo. I—hell." He dropped the cell phone, jammed his foot on the brake pedal, and jerked right on the steering wheel. The pickup careened off the dirt road. Dust, gravel, and tumbleweed flew up and smacked against the windshield, and the jackrabbit he'd swerved to avoid hitting disappeared into the darkness. "Damn," Jack said, his heart pounding madly. He pulled back onto the road and glanced into the pickup's bed to make certain Boozer was all right. The big dog looked at him through the window and barked, obviously fine but not altogether happy with Jack's driving.

Jack snatched up the cell phone. "Maggie?"

"Yeah, you all right, Jack?"

"Yeah. Listen, I got a call from LeeAnn Clay a few minutes ago. She sounded like she might be in trouble."

"Want me to send someone? You know a family was murdered on their ranch up around Four Corners just a few weeks ago, and they haven't caught any suspects yet."

"Great," Jack grumbled; he hadn't needed to be reminded of that. "I'm almost there, Maggie. If you don't hear back from me in ten minutes, figure something's wrong and send someone out on the run."

He hung up and turned his pickup onto the drive leading to the Clay ranch house. Jack knew, from the several other times he'd been there, that it was normally ablaze with light. His uneasiness increased at seeing that the entire place was dark except for a faint light in one downstairs window. He brought the pickup to a skidding stop near the entry walk and threw his door open, jumping to the ground and running to the front door. He banged his fist on it. "LeeAnn? Lee-Ann?" He pounded on the door again.

He was about to run around to the rear of the house when the door opened.

"Jack," LeeAnn said, and smiled. The black negligee she wore clung to her body like a second skin, the sheen of the silk picking up the light from a flickering candle on a table beside the door, and another on the fireplace mantel in the room beyond the foyer. A long slit on one side of the gown revealed a well-tanned thigh, while the sheer lace that covered her breasts left little to the imagination.

He stared at her, dumbfounded.

"Come in," LeeAnn said softly, brushing her long white-blonde hair from her shoulders.

"You . . . you said . . ." Jack swallowed hard in an effort to move past his shock. "You said it was an emergency."

LeeAnn smiled. "Did I?" A throaty laugh slipped from her lips. "Then it must be."

Jack's eyes narrowed as he watched her turn away and walk toward the other room, her hips swaying suggestively. She obviously expected him to follow. Anger erupted deep inside of him, and he stalked after her. "LeeAnn," he practically growled, "it's after nine o'clock. You said it was urgent. What's wrong?"

She set the candle down on a table, then turned and walked back to where he stood, just inside the archway between rooms. Sliding her hands up his chest, she wrapped her arms around him. "It is urgent, Jack," she said huskily, and brushed her lips across his. "I need you, and I couldn't wait any longer."

"LeeAnn," Jack snapped, grabbing her arms and pulling them from around his neck.

The sound of a siren cut through the otherwise silent night. "Ah, hell," Jack swore, realizing he'd forgotten to call Maggie Shallene back.

LeeAnn's eyes hardened as she looked up at him. "Is that your cavalry coming to save you, Jack?"

"No," he snarled, "it's the police coming to save you."

Outside, Boozer sat up in the bed of Jack's pickup and began to howl in accompaniment to the wailing police car that was nearing the house.

Jack ran outside. "Boozer, stop," he ordered, and the dog immediately quieted and lay down. Jack walked up to the police car as it screeched to a halt behind his truck. He leaned down beside the officer's open window. "It's okay here, Pete," he said. "LeeAnn's alone and thought she heard someone prowling around the place."

"Maybe we'd better have a look," Pete said, and reached for his shotgun.

"I already have. Boozer did too. It was probably just a coyote or something."

Pete's eyes narrowed above the hawklike nose his glasses perched on. "You sure, Jack?"

He nodded. "Sorry to have bothered you."

The deputy grinned, his narrow face barely widening at the movement. "Hell, no bother. It's not often I get to run full out like that with the lights and siren on," he said. "Kinda fun, you know?"

"Yeah. Thanks anyway, Pete. See ya." Jack stepped back from the police car and watched it pull away, then walked back up to the house, where LeeAnn was lazing against the entryway, not having bothered to cover herself with a robe.

She straightened, smiled, and reached out toward

him, but Jack stopped before he came in contact with her hands. "Where's your father?" he asked harshly.

LeeAnn smiled slyly. "Down in Bisbee playing poker. And he's spending the night there, so we've got the whole place to ourselves."

"No, we don't," Jack said. "I was already in bed when you called." He didn't bother telling her he hadn't been in bed alone.

"Which is exactly where I want to be," LeeAnn said. "With you."

Jack took her hands in his. She wasn't going to make this easy. He didn't want to hurt her, but he had to make her understand that what she wanted to happen between them wasn't going to. Ever. "LeeAnn, I can't give you what you want," he said softly.

"Um, yes you can, Jack, just as soon as you get out of those clothes," she whispered, and tried to press herself up against him.

Jack held her firmly away and shook his head. "No. Someday you'll meet a man who'll love you more than you ever thought a man could, and you'll love him. But that man's not me, LeeAnn."

Her arms dropped to her sides as her face hardened in anger. "It's because of *her*, isn't it?"

He knew she meant Kate. "No. It's because it's not right between us."

"It was before she came to town."

He sighed and released her hands. "It wasn't, Lee-Ann, and we both know it."

"You wanted me before she came around."

She would never believe he didn't love her, Jack

realized. Her father had always told her she could have anything she wanted, but she was suddenly finding out that wasn't true. Jack wished he hadn't been the one to make her realize that. He sighed. "I'm sorry, LeeAnn. Good night."

Kate entered the kitchen.

"Oh, good morning, Kate," Marion said. "Look, Violet's blooming. I think my little pep talk the other day and that new plant food I gave her was just what she needed."

Kate smiled and looked at the plant Marion was holding. "She's beautiful. Looks like she took your words to heart."

Marion set the plant back on the windowsill and pulled a tray of sweet rolls from the oven. "Did you sleep well?"

"Yes, thanks." Kate poured herself a cup of coffee and was about to sit down at the table when Liz entered the room.

"Morning, everyone," she said, heading directly for the refrigerator. She took a can of soda from one of its shelves.

"Lizzie, however can you drink that horrible stuff so early in the morning?" Marion asked.

"Easy. It's good," she quipped, and held the can out toward her mother. "You should try it."

"Yuck." Marion wrinkled her nose in distaste.

Liz sat down at the table opposite Kate, grabbed a

sweet roll, then turned back toward her mother. "Hey, Mom, is Jack home?"

"Of course, dear, why wouldn't he be?" Marion pulled a small devil's ivy plant from the window and stuck a finger into the soil. "Oh, you need some breakfast, too, don't you, little one?"

Liz shrugged. "Well, you never know. I mean, I heard him drive off last night and figured he was going to LeeAnn's"—she shrugged—"so I thought maybe he decided to stay."

Kate stiffened. After he'd left her last night she hadn't gone back to sleep, at least not in his bed. Instead she'd gone to her own room and read awhile before falling asleep.

Marion continued to murmur to her plant and poke a finger around in its soil.

Liz turned to Kate. "They've been dating for the last several months," she said. "LeeAnn told me they've even started talking about marriage."

"Grandma." Tiffany charged into the room looking flustered. "I can't find my bracelet."

Marion looked up. "What bracelet, dear?"

"My bracelet," she wailed, throwing herself down on a chair. "The gold one Daddy gave me for my birthday."

Marion set the plant back on the windowsill and then bent down to rummage about under the sink. "It's probably in that mess on your dresser."

"No, it's not, I looked."

"Clean your room, dear," Marion said, "I'm sure you'll find it."

"It's not there," Tiffany said. "I left it on my night-stand last night and now it's not there."

"Oh, here you are," Marion said, smiling as she rose with a fertilizer stick in her hands. "Ivy's breakfast."

"Grandma," Tiffany wailed again.

Marion looked at her. "Eat a sweet roll, dear. And don't forget to drink some juice."

Kate stood and walked to the open back door. A moment later she heard Jack greet his mother as he entered the kitchen, but she kept her back to him and remained at the door, staring out at the mountains in the distance.

They'd made love twice, and both times had been a mistake. The first time he'd left her because he'd been angry at a reference she'd made to her past. The second time he'd left her to go to LeeAnn Clay.

Kate sighed and pushed the unpleasant thoughts aside. She didn't want to think about them, or Jack Ringo. Her gaze roamed slowly over the landscape spread out before her. So much had changed, except the mountains.

"Good morning, Kate," Jack said, moving up beside her and reaching for the coffeepot on the counter.

"Good morning." She turned and walked toward the door to the hall. "I'd better get ready for work."

Jack watched her leave. Great. She was mad at him again.

"Tiffany's gold bracelet is missing, Jack," Liz said, drawing his attention.

He looked at his sister. "So? She'll find it."

Liz's brows rose dramatically. "Will she?"

His temper flared. He was in no mood for this. Not after what had happened with LeeAnn. And now finding out Kate was mad at him again. "Look, Liz—"

"No, you look," she said, barely above a whisper, "things are disappearing around here, Jack, and that never happened before she came."

"Elizabeth," Marion said.

Liz looked at her mother. "Have you found your gold earrings, Mom? Or your brooch?"

Marion frowned. "Well, no."

"And none of the other things have turned up either. Now Tiffany's gold bracelet is missing." She looked back at Jack. "A little much for coincidence, I'd say. Maybe you'd better check down at Carney's shop, big brother, and see if anyone's sold him any jewelry lately."

Jack walked out of the room without answering. He didn't want to think about Liz's accusation. The problem was, he couldn't help himself. He might not like it, but she was right. Too many things had turned up missing for it to be mere coincidence, and none of them had disappeared before Kate's arrival.

SIXTEEN

Kate closed the door to Jack's office behind her and immediately unzipped the bodice of her dress. She was so uncomfortable, she was about to scream. How the women of this time ever got used to these things, she'd never know. She unhooked the brassiere Liz had loaned her and shrugged out of it. After pulling her dress back on and sighing with relief at how much more comfortable she was, she looked around for her purse. She'd left it under the bar earlier. She couldn't walk out there with a lady's underthing in her hand. Kate folded the garment and slipped it between several books on a small table to one side of Jack's desk. No one was likely to see it there, and she could come back for it at the end of the day.

Jack popped a pretzel into his mouth. "Damned good crowd today," he said to Ben, and looked over the room packed with tourists.

The older man nodded.

"Where's Kate?"

"Went in the back a few minutes ago," Ben said.

The words had no sooner left Ben's lips than Jack caught a flash of red out of the corner of his eye and turned to see Kate coming from the hallway that led to his office. Desire seized him as he watched her walk across the room, the ruffles at the hem of her short satin skirt swaying about her knees, her dark hair cascading over her bare shoulders. He felt the inseam of his pants begin to tighten and rammed his fist into the sinkful of ice he used for the drinks.

Ben jerked around to look at him. "What the . . . ?" Then he spotted Kate, and smiled. "You got it that bad, Jack?"

Jack glowered at him. "I rammed my little finger on the counter is all."

Ben laughed and shook his head. "Yeah. Right."

A few minutes later Liz walked into the Oriental and up to the bar. "I need my earrings," she said to Jack.

"Another party?"

"Yes. Ken's having dinner catered at his place for just me and him. Real fancylike, and I want to wear my earrings."

"Trying to make up to you, huh?" Ben said.

Liz smiled, a devilish gleam in her blue eyes. "He's trying."

Ben chuckled. "Which means he's still got a long way to go."

Jack waved Liz toward his office. "Be back in a minute, Ben."

He knelt down behind his desk and worked the combination lock on the safe, pulling the door open and reaching for the small jewelry box that always sat on the bottom shelf. His hand froze.

"What's the matter?" Liz asked, when he didn't move.

Her voice jerked him out of his stupor, and he grabbed the jewelry box and stood. "Nothing." He handed her the box. "Be careful with these."

"I always am," she said, and slipped the small box into her purse. She looked back at him and frowned. "You sure nothing's wrong? You look kind of funny."

"I'm fine," he managed, and forced himself to smile. It felt more like a grimace, but it was the best he could do at the moment. "Need anything else?" he asked while his mind silently shouted for her to hurry up and leave. He desperately needed to look back in the safe and assure himself that he hadn't seen what he thought he'd seen.

Liz shrugged. "Nope. I'll see you later." She turned to go. "Oh, I almost forgot." She reached into her purse and drew out an envelope and a small, gift-wrapped package. "I was supposed to give you these."

Jack set the package on his desk. "What's this?" He stared at his name written in flourishing script across the envelope. "My birthday's not for several more months."

"Open it and find out." Liz stared at him, a smug

smile tugging at the corners of her lips. "The box first."

Jack set the card down and ripped the paper from the box, then removed its lid. "The eelskin wallet I've been wanting," he said, picking it up.

"Look inside."

He pulled out two airline tickets to Las Vegas, and a faxed copy of a three-day reservation confirmation for a suite at the Mirage, starting for the day after the festival ended. He looked up at his sister, puzzled.

"Open the card, Jack."

He pulled the card from the envelope and read it. *Sorry about last night. See you at the airport, if not before. Love always, LeeAnn.*

Jack looked back up at Liz, about to hand her both the card and wallet and tell her to return them, but she was gone. He sighed. It was probably better he do it himself anyway. Putting the card and wallet aside, he walked across the room and shut his office door. After a moment's hesitation he clicked the lock into place and returned to the safe, hunkering down in front of it and pulling the door open again. He stared at the small red velvet bag with its black silk drawstring. He hadn't imagined it. Even without picking it up, he could tell the bag was empty, and it shouldn't have been.

He picked it up and set it on his desk, then rummaged through everything in the safe. A moment later he had to accept the fact that Johnny Ringo's pocket watch wasn't there.

For the next hour Jack sat at his desk, deep in thought. Yet even as he sat there, mulling everything over in his mind, he knew he had no options. Finally, pushing out of the old swivel chair, he left his office and returned to the saloon.

"Hell, I thought you'd gone off somewhere," Ben said.

"I've got to talk to Kate."

He stared hard at Jack and frowned. "We're real busy right now," he said, which was unusual because Ben always prided himself on being able to handle the bar no matter how busy it got.

"We won't be long." Jack weaved his way through the crowded tables until he reached Kate, who was taking drink orders from a half-dozen happily chatting tourists. "I need to talk to you."

She looked up at him and felt a shiver skip up her spine at the darkness that seemed to emanate from his eyes. At that moment he looked more like Johnny than he ever had. "Okay," she said softly.

"In my office." He turned and walked away.

Kate gave Ben the drink orders, pointed out which table he'd have to take them to, and went to Jack's office. "Is something wrong?" she asked as he motioned her to sit down in the chair before his desk.

"Yes." He slipped the card and gift from LeeAnn into a drawer, but left the empty red bag on his desk. "Have you ever seen that before?" He nodded toward the bag.

Kate glanced at it. "The bag? No, why?"

"A couple of days ago my mother couldn't find a pair of gold earrings."

"I know. Did you find them? Are they in that bag?"

"No."

"Then . . ."

"Jessi can't find her necklace."

Kate nodded. "I helped her look for it."

"Yesterday my mother couldn't find her cameo brooch. And Tiffany's gold bracelet is missing."

Wariness washed over Kate, but she didn't want to believe he was headed in the direction she suspected.

"Yesterday we found the prize money for the shoot-out that the Oriental always sponsors during the festival was missing from my safe." He moved his chair to one side and nodded at the open safe under the table behind the desk.

He was accusing her. She bolted from the chair. "You think I took them," she said, clenching her hands so tightly that her fingernails bit into her flesh. "That I'm a thief."

"And now," Jack went on, his hard gaze holding hers, "Johnny's watch is missing."

Kate looked down at the red bag, his words shocking her and momentarily stilling her fury. "His pocket watch?" she said disbelievingly. "The one with the ruby-and-diamond inset, and the rearing horse engraved on the cover?"

How could she have known? he asked himself. He hardly ever took it out of the safe, so how could she have known what it looked like—unless she'd taken it?

She saw his expression harden at her words, and all her anger and indignation rushed back through her. "How dare you!" she snapped, picking up a paperweight from his desk and slamming it back down again. She whirled around to storm out of the room.

"You were at the house when the things there disappeared," he said, hating himself for the accusation but knowing he had no choice, "and had access to my office here."

Kate stopped and turned, her hands once again clenched into fists. Her eyes glistened with tears, but he found no softness in the dark blue depths at the moment, only fury and resentment. "I may have been a lot of things in my life, Jack Ringo," Kate said, her tone fiery with anger, "but I was never a thief, and even if I was, I would never, ever steal anything from the man I love. Or his family!"

Whirling about again, Kate ran from the room.

Shocked by her words, Jack stared for several long moments at the empty doorway, then finally bolted from his chair and out into the saloon.

"Jack," Liz said, walking up to him. "It's time for your big showdown with Wyatt Earp."

He looked at her, puzzled; he'd thought she had left.

"Come on, your audience is waiting," she said, and laughed. She held out his hat, gun, and holster. "Time to show everyone what a Ringo is really made of."

He looked around the saloon, but there was no sign of Kate. Jack glanced toward Ben.

"She left," he said, as if reading Jack's mind.

"Jack." Liz pushed the holster and gun at him. "Come on."

He'd have to find Kate later. Slamming the hat

onto his head, he strapped on the holster, checked his gun, then walked outside and lazed against one of the overhanging roof's support beams, waiting for his cue.

A few minutes later a hush came over the tourists gathered on the boardwalks as a tall man in a long black frock coat and flat-brimmed hat, sporting a handlebar mustache, appeared from around the corner of the Birdcage Theatre. He walked out into the center of the street and slowly began to approach Jack.

"I told you to get out of town, Ringo," the man pretending to be Wyatt Earp yelled.

Jack smiled and stepped down off the boardwalk onto the street. "I kinda like it here, Marshal."

"But I don't like you, Ringo."

Jack shrugged. "Can't say as I'm all that fond of you either, Earp."

The other man stopped several yards away, drew back the right side of his frock coat, and hitched it behind the handle of the Peacemaker tied to his thigh. His hand hovered menacingly close to the gun. "Get on your horse and ride, Ringo. It isn't a good day to die."

Jack laughed at the ad-libbed last line, then sobered and moved to the center of the street, standing with his legs spread, his hand only an inch from his gun butt, fingers flexing in readiness. "It's always a good day to die, Marshal," he said, "long as it ain't me doing the dying."

"Damn, hell, and the devil's tarnation," Kate said loudly, drawing everyone's attention and stepping down from the boardwalk to stand directly between the

two men. Boozer lumbered after her. "Is this supposed
to be a walk-down?"

Jack stared at her, taken aback.

"Well, you've got it all wrong," she snapped.
"First"—she glared at Jack—"when two fools want to
kill each other like this, it wasn't called a shoot-out, we
called it a walk-down. And second"—she stomped over
to Jack, hands on her hips and fire spitting from her
eyes—"if you wanted to really hit anything, tie down
your holster, or all you'll shoot is your own foot."

The crowd laughed, the man portraying Wyatt
Earp looked on in clear amusement, and Jack felt his
cheeks start to burn.

"Just what in the hell do you think you're doing?"
he whispered.

"And," Kate continued, ignoring his question,
"Johnny Ringo would have never done a walk-down
without wearing his sash." She slid the red lace shawl
that went with her festival costume off her shoulders
and turned to the crowd. "Johnny Ringo was a member
of the Cowboys," she said loudly, "which was Curly
Bill Brocious's gang, though Johnny gave orders to the
men just as much as Curly did. Anyway, they all wore a
red sash around their hips so everybody would know
they were a Cowboy. It was their sign." She turned
back to Jack and held the shawl out to him.

Jack snatched it from her hand and whipped it
around his hips, tying it with a jerk. "Satisfied?" he
growled under his breath. He glanced down at Boozer.
"Traitor," he muttered.

Kate smiled, then turned back to the onlookers.

"No smart gunman ever wanted to walk toward the sun in a walk-down, unless he didn't have a choice," she said loudly. "But Johnny Ringo didn't care." She looked back at Jack. "He always pulled his hat down low, like this." She reached up and pulled the brim of Jack's hat lower on his forehead. "And the conchas he had on his hatband were to reflect the sun into the other man's eyes."

"Thank you," Jack said loudly. He turned toward the spectators. "Now, folks," he said, holding Kate's arm up by the wrist, "give this little lady a round of applause for all that research she's done for you."

He couldn't have said anything worse. Kate's already burning temper turned volcanic. She jerked her arm away from him.

"The Cowboys never fought fair," she said, before Jack could usher her off the street. "They always had someone standing on a roof or balcony with a rifle."

"Thank you again," Jack said, nearly shouting this time. He started to urge her toward the boardwalk, his hand on her back giving her little choice. "We'll talk later," he said. Once she was in front of the Oriental, he turned and walked back to the center of the street to face down "Wyatt Earp."

"Oh, and Johnny and Wyatt never did face each other down like this," Kate said. "Doc killed Johnny out in one of the canyons a few miles from town." With that, she turned and disappeared into the crowd.

Jack stared after her. If he'd ever wanted to wring a woman's neck, he wanted to do it now.

SEVENTEEN

After walking the streets for over an hour, Jack finally spotted Kate at the edge of town staring out over an empty patch of land. He knew that there had been buildings there, blocks of them, when the town had been a thriving metropolis in the middle of the desert. But that had been a long time ago, and at the moment the history of the town he'd grown up in wasn't uppermost in his mind.

"What the hell was that all about?" he said, grabbing her arm and whirling her around to face him.

"The truth," she said. "Though I doubt you'd know it if it reared up and slapped you in the face."

"Yeah, well, maybe if you'd try telling it once in a while, I'd believe it."

She jerked away from him. "I have."

"Yeah, right. I'm supposed to believe all this stuff you've been spouting about being the real Kate Holliday, Doc Holliday's mistress. How you knew my great-great-great-grandfather, and all the others." He felt his head throb from the heat of his temper. "And what was all that garbage about in the street back there? You nearly ruined the whole damned show, saying Johnny and Wyatt never faced each other down."

"They didn't."

"Oh, right, I forgot, you were there," he said with a sneer. "You'd know. Just like you know for a fact that Johnny Ringo never fought fair."

"I didn't say Johnny," Kate spat, "I said the Cowboys."

"Of which he was one."

"That's right." Her own temper flared. "Stop glorifying Johnny and all the others, Jack," she snapped. "Ike Clanton was a coward, Curly Bill was a damned bully, and Johnny Ringo was an arrogant son-of-a . . . and all too quick to pull his trigger against anyone. He killed people just for looking at him wrong. He was handsome and smart and charming, but he was also a cold-blooded killer."

"Oh, damn." Jack threw his hands up in the air. "This is useless."

She turned her back to him. "We used to live here," she said softly. "Right here. This is where our house was, mine and Doc's, before it burned down. The fire started in the saloon just a few doors down from the Oriental, you know?" She turned back to look up at Jack. "We stayed in the Palace Hotel after that."

He glared at her, unable to believe she was still going on with her game.

"And I wasn't Doc's mistress, Jack. I told you, I was his wife. His common-law wife."

"Jeez Almighty, what do you take me for, Kate, a fool?"

"No."

"Then tell me the truth."

"I have."

"You haven't told me anything a good researcher couldn't have found out. Everything you've said is in one history book or another." *Except for the description of Johnny Ringo's pocket watch*, a little voice in the back of his mind whispered. He ignored it. She could describe the watch, if she'd stolen it. "Prove your claims, Kate," Jack challenged, wishing he believed she could. "If you're telling the truth, prove it."

She stared at him. "How?"

His brows soared mockingly, but he remained silent.

Suddenly Kate smiled and whirled away from him.

"Where are you going?" he called after her.

"To get your proof." If she was lucky, the box would still be where she'd left it. She ran back into town and down its main street, weaving hurriedly around the tourists until she got to the old building that had once been the Palace Hotel. When she and Doc had lived there, the first floor had consisted of small shops and the lobby of the hotel. Now the first floor sported a sign over the door that declared it . . . she smiled to herself . . . Big-nosed Kate's Saloon.

She rushed into the saloon and ran toward the stairs in the rear.

"Hey, lady, nobody's supposed to go up there," the bartender yelled.

She ignored him. At the landing she turned left and hurried toward the room at the rear. The carpet had been removed from the hall, as well as the pictures she remembered that had graced the walls. And the crystal chandelier over the landing was gone. She prayed the box wasn't.

Pausing in front of the door that had once been the entry to the room she'd shared with Doc for the last few months of their relationship, Kate said a little prayer. It had been a long time since she'd done that, but then it had been a long time since anything in her life had mattered as much as Jack Ringo did. She knew that whether she was allowed to stay in this time or not, she needed to prove to him that she wasn't a thief and a liar. Because she loved him, she wanted him to be able to believe her.

She turned the handle, and as the door swung open she stepped into the room. Fear clutched at her heart. She didn't know what she'd expected, but she hadn't expected the room to be empty. There wasn't a stick of furniture in it. The walls were water-stained and gray with age, and what paint was left on them was peeling. The curtains on the windows were little more than shreds of rotting lace, and the wood floor was bare of carpet, dull, scratched, and warped. But a momentary flash of memory showed Kate the room the way it had once been. She remembered the ornate bed's tall, elegantly carved headboard, a green-brocade-covered settee and matching chair, a marble-topped table upon which had been a crystal lamp. The curtains had been snowy white with green brocade tiebacks, and a bureau with a flowered water pitcher and washbowl had been beside the wall next to the closet door. The door stood open. Kate swallowed hard, pushed her memories to the back of her mind where they belonged, and felt her hopes sink further as she stared into the dark interior of the closet. Had someone found it? Had someone taken the small box she'd forgotten the night she'd left Tombstone and Doc?

Kate took a hesitant step into the room. The floor creaked beneath her weight, and the sound sent her running toward the closet. She swung the door back farther, slamming it against the wall, so that more light poured into the small cavity. Stepping to the rear wall, she dropped to her knees and began pressing on the wood edging at the floor. "Where is it?" she mumbled to herself as her fingers moved and pressed, moved and pressed. "Where is it?"

Suddenly the molding gave a bit beneath her fingers. Kate pushed harder and felt it move again. "Yes." She laughed, her excitement and her hopes soaring. She pushed again, as hard as she could, but the wood barely moved this time.

She had never trusted banks, so when they'd moved into the Palace Doc had cut a foot of molding from the closet's rear wall and hollowed out a little square for her to place her valuables in. Kate sat back and looked at it. It had been painted over several times and was obviously stuck. She looked around for something to pry it open with, but saw nothing. Scrambling to her feet, she looked into the room next door, then another and another. They were all empty, but finally, in the last one she checked, she saw a stack of tarps, several cans of paint, brushes, and something that looked like a very fat, very square knife with a red handle. Grabbing it, she hurried back to the closet.

A few seconds later the molding fell away from the wall and Kate gasped.

After trying to figure out where Kate had run off to, Jack gave up and returned to the Oriental. He sat down behind his desk and stared once again at the little red velvet bag that lay before him. "Damn." He kicked the metal trash can beside his desk with the heel of his boot. The can flew across the room and clattered against the leg of the table where he kept his books. The table shook, the books fell, and Kate's brassiere tumbled into view.

Jack stared at it. "Where the hell did that come from?" But as soon as the words left his lips, he was pretty sure he knew the answer. That was the reason why Kate had been in his office. He remembered his mother laughing the day before when she'd told him, evidently believing everything Kate claimed about herself, how funny she found it that Kate couldn't stop complaining about wearing a bra, saying it felt like someone was trying to squeeze her breasts to death.

Jack wasn't as willing as his mother to believe that Kate had never had to wear a bra, but he was willing to believe that she hadn't taken the watch and the money.

Jack knew it was a long shot, that the odds were she'd come into his office with the excuse of removing the bra *and* had stolen the money and watch, but he wanted to believe in the long shot.

Kate pulled the box from its hiding place in the wall and set it on her lap. She was almost afraid to open it. What if it was empty? But why would Doc, or anyone else, have put the box back into its hiding place if they'd emptied it?

Maybe Doc had forgotten about it, too, and no one else had ever found it.

There was only one way to find out if the things she'd left in the box were still there.

She scooted from the closet into the big empty room and, with shaking fingers, lifted the box's lid. The first thing she saw was her small lemonwood jewelry box. She lifted it from the dust-covered metal box and removed its delicately inlaid top. The diamond pendant and earrings Doc had given her just before they'd left Wichita sparkled in the sunlight shining into the room. Kate gasped at seeing them again, and tears filled her eyes. She remembered how Doc had laughed when he'd given them to her and said that he'd bought them because they had reminded him of her, cold and hard, but with a fire burning deep inside that only a privileged few would ever be allowed to see and feel. At the time his words had hurt, had dulled the excitement she'd felt at receiving his gift, but after a while she'd

come to understand what he'd meant and even agree
with him.

She'd been that way so long, holding her real self
off from most people, using them for her own needs
because she'd had to in order to survive, that she'd
never seen those things in herself.

To some degree, she realized now, she had even
used Jack and his family. She hadn't stolen from them,
but she had used them. Unlike the other times when
she used people, she really did care about Jack Ringo
and his "girls."

Pushing those thoughts aside, Kate closed the small
jewelry box and lifted out a cache of IOUs made out to
Doc by various people who'd lived in Tombstone and
who had been foolish enough to gamble with him. If
he'd wanted, he probably could have owned half the
town. Beneath the IOUs was a stack of greenbacks.
Kate smiled as she thumbed through the large old bills,
mentally comparing them with the money people used
now. A pearl-handled derringer, the mate of the one
she'd lost in the stagecoach crash, was still nestled in a
corner of the box, the pair a gift from Doc. But rather
than lift it out, she gathered up the stack of old daguerreotypes lying next to it. The one on top was of
Doc. She smiled as she looked at it.

"You never thought anyone would remember you,"
she said softly, "but you were wrong, Doc. Everyone
remembers you. And Wyatt, and Virgil, and Morgan,
and all the others." She blinked back the tears that had
filled her eyes and began to shuffle through the other
old pictures until she came to the one she'd been look-

ing for. Kate held it up, and as sunlight touched the picture and lit up the faces of the people whose images had been caught there forever, a sense of nostalgia swept over her and tugged at her heart. They were all gone now, but she would never forget them. This was what she'd hoped, above all other things, was still in the box. This is what would prove to Jack that she was telling the truth.

Hurriedly putting everything else back into the box, Kate stood and walked from the room, but at the landing she paused.

"I told her she couldn't go up there, Sheriff, but she did anyway. I would have gone up after her myself, but I didn't have anyone else here to take over the bar."

"Okay. I'll go on up and see what's going on."

EIGHTEEN

Kate looked about frantically. She couldn't let the sheriff see the box, he might take it away from her. But she couldn't leave it there either. She might not be able to get back in to get it again. Then she remembered the rear stairs, the ones the hotel's staff had used. She bolted across the hall and opened the door opposite the room she'd just left. The steep and narrow stairway was black as pitch, but she had no choice. It was the only way out. Stepping past the door, she quietly closed it behind her, and feeling the wall with one hand and holding the box to her side with the other, she began to make her way down in the dark, praying none of the stairs were rotten. She didn't want to have traveled a hundred and sixteen years only to fall in love and then die. And if she fell here and broke her neck, the likelihood was, judging from the condition of the upstairs rooms and the spiderwebs she kept running into, no one would ever find her.

What seemed like an eternity later, Kate finally stepped off the last stair and rammed her face into the door that gave access to the rear of the hotel.

Pushing it open, she stepped out into the sunlight, took a deep breath to rid her lungs of the mustiness of the enclosed stairwell, and blinked at the glare of light that assaulted her eyes. She looked down at the red satin dress she still wore. It was covered with dust, a cobweb clung to the toe of her right shoe, and if she wasn't mistaken—she shuddered—another was caught in her hair. She hoped its maker hadn't accompanied his home's move. Kate bent over and shook her head vigorously, then ran her fingers through her hair. She slapped at her skirt, brushed the cobweb from her shoe, and glanced in a nearby window. What she could see of herself didn't look too bad. She shook her head again, then hurried away before the sheriff could spot her.

Pushing past the Oriental's swinging doors, she walked directly to the bar and stopped before Jack. She set the box in front of him. "I have your proof."

He looked from Kate to the box. Whatever she had in there, he had a feeling, judging from the age of the box, didn't need to be seen by everyone in the room. "Ben, take over," he said, "We're going to my office. Be back in a few minutes." He grabbed a towel before going.

Boozer, spotting Kate, slowly got to his feet and lumbered after her.

She set the metal box on Jack's desk as he closed the door behind them, then walked around the desk to face her. He handed her the towel.

"What's this for?" Kate asked.

"That smudge of dirt on your cheek."

She wiped it off.

Jack turned his attention to the box. "What's this?"

"The proof you asked for."

He sat down.

"Several months before I left town, the house Doc and I shared burned down."

"So you said."

"We took a room at the Palace Hotel, though why we were staying together by then, I don't know. We were fighting a lot, and Doc was drinking more than he usually did. Anyway, the only thing that survived the fire, besides us and the clothes we had on our backs at the time, was this box and what was inside of it."

"Was?" Jack said.

"Is." She opened its lid and took out the stack of IOUs, dropping them in front of Jack. "These are IOUs I had been holding for Doc."

Jack shuffled through them. They looked old, looked authentic, but that didn't really mean anything. There were a lot of old documents for sale in the world, and he wasn't a collector, so just because he hadn't heard of them didn't mean they didn't exist. He recognized the names of several families still in the area. He looked back at Kate, waiting for her to go on.

She handed him the greenbacks, left the derringer and the other old daguerreotypes in the box, and pulled out only the one she hoped would convince him she'd been telling the truth. Holding the picture in her hand, Kate stared down at it for several long seconds, her thoughts again on what might have happened if she hadn't left town that day.

"What's that?" Jack asked.

She took a deep breath and handed him the picture.

Jack's gaze moved slowly from one face in the picture to the next. He recognized the Earps instantly, Wyatt and Josie, Virgil, Morgan, and their wives. He even recognized Buckskin Frank Leslie and Luke Short, two more of Wyatt's friends, and men who'd worked for him in the Oriental.

As his gaze moved from Doc Holliday to the woman standing beside him, the breath caught in his throat and he froze, even his heartbeat seeming to pause in shock. He knew there was a logical explanation for what he was seeing.

"That's all of us standing in front of the Oriental," Kate said, "just after Wyatt took it over."

Jack stared at the woman in the old picture who was the spitting image of Kate. He looked up. "You're a descendant," he said, still unwilling to believe anything else was possible. "Just like me."

Kate sighed and shook her head. "Do you have a magnifying glass?"

He pulled one from the drawer and held it out to her.

Kate shook her head again. "No, you use it. Look at that picture of me . . . of Kate Holliday."

He positioned the magnifying glass over the picture.

"What do you see on her neck?" Kate asked softly. "Off to one side."

Jack moved the glass up and down to get better focus. He paused and stared. "It looks like a spot." He looked up at Kate, then back at the picture. "It's shaped kind of like a moon."

"Like this?" Kate brushed her hair aside and turned so that he could see the crescent-shaped birthmark.

Jack stared at it. "But how . . ." he said, unable to finish his own question.

"It's always been there."

"No." He felt dazed. "How could this have happened? How could you have been there . . . and be here too?"

"I don't know," Kate whispered, still afraid to believe that he had accepted her truth. "One minute I was on the stagecoach, Indians were chasing us, and we toppled over a cliff. The next thing I knew I was lying in your cactus garden."

Jack closed his eyes and shook his head. "No, that's impossible."

"Then you tell me what happened," she said, an edge of anger and frustration in her tone, as well as challenge. "Who am I, Jack? Where am I from? How did I get here?"

He opened his eyes and looked at the picture again, then back up at Kate. "This is really you?" he asked. But he didn't need an answer. Something deep down, in the center of his gut, told him that what she'd been saying all along was true. She was Kate Holliday. *The* Kate Holliday.

Fear suddenly seized his heart like a monster reaching out of the darkness. Standing abruptly, he walked around his desk and pulled Kate into his arms. "But what happens now?" he whispered, his lips against her hair. He couldn't lose her. Until that very moment he hadn't known how much she'd come to mean to him, not until the thought of losing her forever slammed into him. "What happens now?"

"I don't know." Kate slipped her arms around his waist. She knew what he was asking. The same question that had been haunting her, the one that had made her fight desperately not to fall in love with him. But she didn't have an answer.

"Dad, Dad." Tiffany's voice filled the hallway. A second later she barged into the room. "Dad, Grandma says you have to come home right away."

He tore away from Kate and grabbed Tiffany, suddenly afraid for another reason now. "What's wrong?"

She gulped in a deep breath. "They made me swear not to tell. You're just supposed to come home now. Grandma said to tell you it was really important."

"But not an emergency?"

"No, but she said it was really, really important that you come now."

Jack relaxed somewhat. "How did you get here?"

"Rode my bike."

He smiled. "Then it must be important." He glanced over his shoulder at Kate. "She's too old to ride a bike now, you know."

Kate smiled but remained silent, remembering she'd heard someone call that horrible thing that had almost run her down in the street a "bike." Was Tiffany riding one of those growling, horrid things?

"Okay," Jack said, turning back to his daughter. "Put your bike in the back of the pickup, and we'll be right out."

He looked at Kate after Tiffany had left. "I'm sorry I didn't believe you," he said softly, reaching out to touch her cheek with the tip of his fingers. "But . . ." He shrugged.

She caught his hand and held on to it tightly. "But you do now?"

He sighed. "I think so, but you have to admit it's a hell of a story to believe."

Kate smiled. "I know."

Twenty minutes later they walked into the Ringo house and found the entire family, along with LeeAnn, sitting in the dining room, waiting for them.

Tiffany scrambled onto the empty chair beside Jessi.

"Okay, Mom," Jack said, approaching them, "what's so important that I had to come home early?"

Kate moved to stand beside Jack, Boozer right beside her. She looked down at the table. Spread out before Marion were a variety of items, and Kate felt certain they were the things that had been missing over the past few days.

One item in particular caught her attention and confirmed her thoughts. Johnny Ringo's watch lay next to a gold bracelet Kate guessed was Tiffany's.

She looked at Jack and found he was also staring at the things on the table.

"Where'd you find them?" he asked, picking up the envelope full of money and Johnny's pocket watch.

"In Kate's room," Liz said, "like I told you we probably would."

Kate gasped. "What?"

LeeAnn smiled. "I always knew there was something phony about her."

"We both did." Liz nodded at her friend and then looked back at Jack. Her defiant gaze dared him to challenge her.

"I didn't take them," Kate said, and looked at Jack, waiting for him to defend her.

Instead he turned from the table and walked down the hall toward his own room.

"Kate dear," Marion said, "why don't you sit down and we can talk about this—"

"I didn't take your things," Kate snapped, angry now. "So there's nothing to talk about." Spinning on her heel, she stormed to the room she'd been using and hurriedly gathered what few things she had. Most were clothes borrowed from Liz, but she'd just have to return them later, when she could buy her own. She couldn't very well go back into town naked.

With tears stinging her eyes, and a horrible hurt gnawing at her heart, Kate hugged Boozer and left the house by the French doors in her room, making certain he couldn't follow her.

It was a long walk to town, but at least, since she'd done it upon her arrival, she knew which way to go and how long it would take her to get there. She'd make it back to town before dark.

❖————————❖

Jack stared at Jessi incredulously. "Are you sure about this, honey?"

Jessi nodded. "I saw her take it, Daddy. I woke up and was thirsty, so I went out to the kitchen to get a glass of water, and on the way back I saw Auntie Liz coming out of Tiff's room, and she had Tiff's gold bracelet."

"And the next morning was when Tiffany said it was missing?"

"Yeah. I didn't say anything 'cause I thought Auntie Liz had just borrowed it and would put it back, and I didn't want to get her in trouble. But then today, when LeeAnn came over, I saw them go into Kate's room and . . ." She paused and hung her head, looking down at her toes.

"Go on, Jess, it's okay."

"Well, I wanted to know what they were doing in Kate's room 'cause I knew Kate was at the Oriental with you, so I listened at the door." She looked suddenly panic-stricken. "I know I'm not supposed to do that, Daddy, and I wouldn't have, honest, but—"

"It's okay," he said again, "this time." He reached over and tweaked her on the arm. "You'll never get into trouble for telling me the truth, Jess. Now go on."

"Okay. I heard LeeAnn say that once you were convinced Kate was a thief, you'd be all too ready to marry a nice country girl like her, then she and Liz would be sisters." Jessi wrinkled her nose. "You're not going to marry her, are you, Daddy? I don't think I'd like her for a mom."

"No, I'm not going to marry LeeAnn, but I think I'd better go on back out there and have a little chat with her and your aunt Liz."

"Is Auntie Liz going to hate me now, Daddy?" Jessi asked. "For telling on her and LeeAnn?"

"No, honey. She'll be too busy trying to apologize to me to hate anyone." He paused at the door and looked back at her. "Jess, you like Kate, don't you?"

She smiled. "Yeah. Kate's neat."

Jack chuckled. "Neat," he murmured to himself as he walked down the hall toward the dining room. He'd thought that word went out of vogue years ago.

NINETEEN

Kate passed the old cemetery, but there was no one she wanted to pay her respects to, no one she wanted to remember. A few minutes later she paused in front of an old house not far from the road leading into town. A sign in the front yard said BUCKMAN'S BED & BREAKFAST. She walked up to the front door and knocked.

A woman who had to be one of the thinnest Kate had ever seen answered almost immediately.

"Well, good afternoon," she said cheerily, brushing at the halo of dirty-blonde hair that surrounded her face. "You need a room?"

"Yes," Kate said. "For a few days."

"Sure, honey, come on in. My name's Dottie Buckman. Lucky for you I had some California folks leave early. Some kind of family emergency. Otherwise, with the festival going on and all, I wouldn't have anything to offer you but a cot in the pantry." She laughed.

Kate nodded and followed the woman past a

warmly furnished parlor and down a hall. Unlike the furnishings in the Ringo house, these were from Kate's time. Her *other* time, she reminded herself.

"Here you go," the woman said. "The Pink Room. Sixty dollars a night, and that includes breakfast every morning and sherry and munchies in the evening, if you want. Bath is through that door over there." She pointed across the room. "You're sharing, of course. And I've got lots of brochures on a table in the parlor you can take for sightseeing."

"Thanks," Kate said, "but I'm not sightseeing, I live here. I work at the Oriental." Then again, she most likely didn't work there anymore, she reminded herself.

"Just in between places, honey," Mrs. Buckman asked, "or treating yourself to a stay away from home?"

"The latter," Kate said, not wanting to have to explain.

"Well, make yourself comfy, and if you need anything, just holler." She left, closing the door behind her.

Kate dropped the bag she'd stuffed her clothes into on the floor and lay down on the bed, pulling its pink crocheted coverlet over her. She fell asleep almost instantly.

The sun was just starting to kiss the mountains when she woke. Taking one of the summer sweaters Liz had loaned her from the bag, she threw it around her shoulders, left the house, and began to walk toward town. She didn't know where she was going, all she knew was that she'd never felt so alone in her life, and she needed to be around people.

Reaching Allen Street, she found the boardwalks still crowded with tourists. The fireworks were scheduled for later, marking the end of the festival. Kate wandered aimlessly, then paused before an old building she recognized. Once it had been one of the most famous restaurants in town. She looked in the window. Now it was some kind of photo studio, with a claw-footed bathtub sitting against one wall, a small bar against another, part of a rail fence, and an old settee. A rack full of old clothes stood near the settee.

Kate turned away and kept walking. What was she going to do now? She knew of no way to get back to her own time, to Doc and Wyatt and everyone she knew, and there was no one here she could turn to for help.

Thoughts of Jack filled her mind. She loved him more than she'd ever loved anyone in her life, but even if he believed her now about who she was, he also believed she was a thief. The pain that assailed her at that thought was almost more than she could bear, and she tried to push all thoughts of Jack Ringo from her mind, even for a little while.

Moving past the photo studio, she passed several buildings she didn't recognize, and then paused before the entry to the O.K. Corral. She remembered what she'd read about it being the place Doc, Wyatt, and his brothers had faced down the Clantons and the McLowerys as she stared at the sign over the door. She wasn't aware of deciding to go in, but a moment later she was walking past several old carriages parked beneath an overhanging roof, and then she was in a wide-open area, like a corral. Several men stood about, and Kate was going to leave, not wanting to bother them, when she realized they weren't real. She approached one and stood in front of it. They were dummies, dressed and painted to look like men—to look like Doc, the Earps, the Clantons, and McLowerys, she suddenly realized. She turned and walked up to the one she knew was supposed to be Doc. It wasn't a very good likeness.

Suddenly someone walked through the entry. He stood in the shadows, watching her. Kate froze, practically hugging the dummy as she realized she was alone with this man, and a good distance from the street and the crowds. She reached to her thigh for the derringer, then remembered she'd lost it when the stagecoach crashed. She also realized that if she screamed, no one would hear her.

"I've been looking everywhere for you," Jack said, stepping out of the darkness and walking toward her. "I must have driven up and down the road into town several times."

"I didn't stay on the road," Kate said.

"I know." He reached out and drew her to him.

"No," Kate said, and tried to push away.

"No," Jack echoed, through with letting Kate slip away from him. His mouth descended on hers before she knew it.

For several very long moments she gave herself up to him, to the pleasure of his kiss. Then reality flashed back upon her, and she tore her lips from his. "No," she said again. "You think I'm a—"

"I think—no." Jack smiled. "I *know* you're the woman I love, and if you had stayed at the house instead of running off and making me go half-crazy searching for you, I would have told you that there."

"But you think I'm a thie—"

"No, I never did." Jack tightened his arms around her, crushing her mercilessly against his body. "Not really. And if you'd stayed at the house you would have heard me tell LeeAnn and Liz that I knew they'd taken all that stuff, not you."

"*They* took it?" Kate echoed, confused.

"Yes."

"But why?"

"LeeAnn is a good five years older than my sister; nevertheless, they've been best friends for several years. LeeAnn fancied herself in love with me, and they got it into their heads that LeeAnn and I would eventually get married."

"You dated her," Kate said, not certain she wanted to hear the rest.

"Yes, and that was a mistake I've been trying to correct for weeks, but LeeAnn only hears what she wants to hear. Anyway, when you showed up on our doorstep, I guess my attraction to you was just a bit too obvious for them, and they decided to do something about it, like get rid of you or turn me against you."

"So they stole those things and tried to make it look like I did," Kate said.

"Yes."

"And you believed them."

He shook his head. "No. I suspected you, I admit, yet I could never bring myself to believe that you'd done it."

"How did you find out it was Liz and LeeAnn?"

"Jessi told me. That's why she called me away from the table."

"I thought you'd walked off because you were angry," Kate said. "At me."

Jack smiled. "I was angry all right, but"—he brushed a kiss across the tip of her nose—"it was never with you."

"Never?" Kate said, laughing.

Jack chuckled. "Well, not that time, anyway." He suddenly turned serious. "I want you to stay, Kate. So does everyone else."

"Not Liz," Kate reminded him.

"She'll get over it. Anyway, she's going back to school and will be living up in Tucson."

Kate shook her head. She wanted to stay with him more than anything, but it wasn't fair to him. What if she was suddenly yanked away from him and sent back to her own time? Or some other time?

"My mother desperately wants you for a daughter-in-law, Kate, and my girls are positively bonkers over you. I know they'd love you to be their stepmother."

"Jack, no, I—"

"And I definitely want you to be my wife," he said softly, his voice husky with emotion.

Pulling away from him took all the willpower she possessed. "It's not right," Kate said, turning her back

to him. "We can't." Tears filled her eyes, and she
fought them back as the most horrible pain she had
ever felt suddenly welled up inside of her and settled
around her heart.

"Why?" Jack demanded. He closed his hands
gently over her shoulders and forced her to turn back
to him. "I know you love me, Kate. Don't you?"

"Yes, I love you, but you don't believe who I really
am, where I came from, and—"

Jack laughed, relieved. "Sweetheart, a lot of people
might think I'm crazy if they heard me say this, and I
don't know when it finally sank into my brain that you
were telling the truth, but I most definitely do believe
you. I don't know how it happened, what brought you
here or why, I'm only damned thankful that it did."

Kate looked up at him, wanting to throw herself
into his arms and stay there for the rest of her life. But
she knew she couldn't. She shook her head. "What
brought me here might come back and . . . take me
away, Jack, and that wouldn't be fair to you and the
girls."

"And it might not come back, Kate. We can't live in
fear, we can't throw away a life together because of
what might or might not happen." He caressed her
cheek lightly. "Marry me, Kate."

She wanted to say yes, she desperately wanted to
say yes. Instead she said, "What about Doc?"

"Doc?" Jack frowned in puzzlement. "What about
him? He's dead." He saw the sudden pain that flashed
across her face and silently cursed himself for putting it
so insensitively. He reached for her again, but she

stepped back. "I'm sorry, Kate, I shouldn't have said it like that."

She shook her head. "You hate him, Jack, because he killed Johnny. Because he killed the man who was your great-great-great-grandfather. But I loved Doc. Not as much as I love you, never as much as I love you, but I did love him. He was my husband. And he was a good man."

"And Johnny Ringo got what he deserved," Jack said. "I know that. I think I've always known it. I just didn't like admitting it."

Kate looked up, surprised. The look in his eyes erased the last shred of doubt in her mind. Turning away, she walked back to the dummy of Doc and stood before it, looking up into his face. She remained there for several long minutes, remembering the man she had spent several years with, the man she had taken care of when he was sick, followed from town to town whenever he grew restless or saw greener pastures just over the hill, feared for when he faced a man down, and loved even when he'd made it so hard. Reaching out, Kate laid a hand upon the lapel of the dummy's coat. But it was no longer a plaster dummy she saw through her tears, but the man himself.

"You've finally found your place in the world, Kate," Doc whispered.

Kate smiled and nodded. Yes, she'd finally found her place in the world, and a man she loved more than anything on earth. "Thank you, Doc," Kate whispered. "And good-bye."

Turning back to Jack, Kate smiled and flung herself into his arms. "I love you, Jack Ringo."

He looked down at her and smiled widely. "Does that mean you'll marry me?"

"Yes," she cried. "Oh, yes."

"Tomorrow?" Jack asked.

"Even tonight."

Jack laughed. "Then let's go find my girls and the preacher, sweetheart, because we've got a wedding to go to."

He grabbed her hand and started for the street, but Kate held back. Jack paused, suddenly afraid she'd changed her mind. "What?" he said hesitantly.

"Would you mind . . . I mean, if we have children . . . a son, would you mind if we named him John."

"John?" Jack repeated. "You mean after . . ."

"After Doc," Kate said. She slipped her arm around Jack's and held on to him tightly. "He always told me I was living in the wrong time, Jack, that my real world was waiting for me out there somewhere." She glanced back at the plaster dummy. "And he was right."

EPILOGUE

Kate tried to shift her position on the sofa, but it didn't help. She felt like a whale. Her stomach was so big, she couldn't even see her feet when she stood. She should have had her shape back by now. The baby was late. But then what wasn't? The baby was late, the flowers she'd ordered for Marion were late, the book was late, and the contractors who were putting in a pool were late every morning. And at least two weeks behind schedule.

"Want something, sweetheart?" Jack asked, walking into the room. He leaned down over the back of the sofa and nuzzled her neck, slipping his hand over her stomach at the same time and caressing it gently.

The baby kicked.

"Whoa, either he doesn't like me doing that," Jack said, and laughed, "or he's restless to come out."

"Well, I wish he'd hurry up," Kate said. "If I get any bigger, I think I might explode."

"You look beautiful."

She laughed, looking down at the yellow maternity pants and top Marion had bought for her. "Oh, right. Like a monstrous swollen lemon."

"Beautiful," Jack said again, pulling her collar back and trailing a series of kisses across her shoulder.

"Ow," Kate cried.

Jack jumped back. "What?"

"I think . . . Ow!"

Jack spun around and ran for their room. She'd been having pains all day and she was a week overdue. He grabbed her coat and suitcase and ran back into the family room, yelling for his mother along the way.

Marion appeared at the kitchen door, a bowl of cookie batter in her hands. "Jacky, for mercy sakes, what are you bellowing about? You're going to give poor Violet a wilting attack."

"It's time," he said. "We're going to the hospital."

"Well, go ahead," Marion said. "Land sakes alive, it's not as if you've never gone through this before."

"Call us when the baby comes," Tiffany called.

The girls gathered on the porch and waved them off as they drove away.

· Three hours later John Lee Ringo made his entry into the world, and let out a wailing scream at the doctor who had the audacity to slap him on his little rear end.

The next morning Jack walked into Kate's hospital room, a vase full of flowers in one hand and a gift-wrapped box in the other. He looked at his son, sleeping peacefully next to Kate, set the flowers on her nightstand, leaned over and kissed a sleeping John Lee lightly on the forehead, then captured Kate's lips in a kiss that made her wish they were home and in their own bed.

"I miss you," he said huskily.

She laughed. "I've only been here since last night."

"Which is far too long to be away from me." He handed her the present.

"What's this?"

"Open it and find out."

Kate tore the wrapping away and stared at the book he'd brought her. *The Life of Dr. John Holliday*, by Kate Holliday-Ringo. She'd had to pretend to be merely a descendant of Doc's in order to sell the book, but she didn't care. She wanted people to know there had been more to Doc than just a gambler, drinker, and killer, and now they would.

"They were just putting them on the shelves when I walked into the bookstore," Jack said.

She looked up at her husband and reached for his hand. "I love you, Jack Ringo. I love you so much."

"And I love you, Kate Holliday-Ringo. More than you'll ever know."

THE EDITORS' CORNER

Men. We love 'em, we hate 'em, but when it comes right down to it, we can't get along without 'em. Especially the ones we may never meet: those handsome guys with the come-hither eyes, those gentle giants with the hearts of gold, those debonair men who make you want to say yes. Well, this October you'll get your chance to meet those very men. Their stories make up LOVESWEPT's MEN OF LEGEND month. There's nothing like reuniting with an old flame, and the men our four authors have picked will definitely have you shivering with delight!

Marcia Evanick presents the final chapter in her White Lace & Promises trilogy, **HERE'S LOOKIN' AT YOU**, LOVESWEPT #854. Morgan De Witt promised his father that he would take care of his sister, Georgia. Now that Georgia's happily engaged, he's facing a lonely future and has decided it's time to find a Mrs. De Witt. Enter Maddie Andrews. Years ago, Maddie offered Morgan her heart, and he rebuffed the gawky fifteen-year-old. Morgan can't understand why Maddie is so aloof, but he's determined to crack her defenses, even if he has to send her the real Maltese Falcon to do so. Maddie's heart melts every time he throws in a line or two from her favorite actor, but can she overcome the fears bedeviling her every thought of happiness? As usual, Marcia Evanick delights readers with a love that is at times difficult, but always, always enduring.

Loveswept favorite Sandra Chastain returns with **MAC'S ANGELS: SCARLET LADY,** LOVE-SWEPT #855. Rhett Butler Montana runs his riverboat casino like the rogue he was named for, but when a mysterious woman in red breaks the bank and then dares him to play her for everything he owns, he's sorely tempted to abandon his Southern gentility in favor of a little one-on-one. With her brother missing and her family's plantation at stake, Katie Carithers has her own agenda in mind; she must form an uneasy alliance with the gambler who's bound by honor to help any damsel in distress. As the two battle over integrity, family, and loyalty, Katie and Rhett discover that what matters most is not material but intangible—that thing called love. Sandra Chastain ignites a fiery duel of wits and wishes when she sends a sexy rebel to do battle with his leading lady.

Next up is Stephanie Bancroft's delightful tale of Kat McKray and James Donovan, the former British agent who boasts a **LICENSE TO THRILL,** LOVESWEPT #856. Even though James Donovan is known the world over as untouchable and hard to hold, he has never lacked for companionship of the female persuasion. But after delivering a letter of historic consequence to the curvaceous museum curator, James is sure his sacred state of bachelorhood is doomed. Kat refuses to lose her heart to another love 'em and leave 'em kind of guy, a vow that slowly dissolves in the wake of James's presence. When Kat is arrested in the disappearance of the valuable artifact, it's up to James to save Kat's reputation and find the true culprit. In a romantic caper that taps into every woman's fantasy of 007 in hot pursuit, Stephanie keeps the pulse racing with a woman desperate to clear her name and that of the spy who loves her.

Talk about a tall tale! Donna Kauffman delivers **LIGHT MY FIRE**, LOVESWEPT #857, a novel about a smoke jumper and a maverick agent whose strength and determination are matched only by each other's. Larger than life, 6′ 7″ T. J. Delahaye rescues people for a living and enjoys it. By no means a shrinking violet at 6′ 2″, Jenna King rescues the environment and is haunted by it. But you know what they say—the bigger they are, the harder they fall—and these two are no exception. Trapped by the unrelenting forces of nature, Jenna and T. J. must rely on instinct and each other to survive. Sorrow has touched them both deeply, and if they make it through this ordeal alive, will they put aside the barriers long enough to learn the secret thrill of surrender? In a story fiercely erotic and deeply moving, Donna draws the reader into an inferno of emotion and fans the flames high with the heat of heartbreaking need.

Happy reading!

With warmest regards,

Susann Brailey   Joy Abella

Susann Brailey   Joy Abella

Senior Editor   Administrative Editor

P.S. Look for these Bantam women's fiction titles coming in October. From Jane Feather, Patricia Coughlin, Sharon & Tom Curtis, Elizabeth Elliott, Patricia Potter, and Suzanne Robinson comes **WHEN YOU WISH . . .** , a collection of truly romantic tales, in which a mysterious bottle containing one wish falls into the hands of each of the heroines . . . with magical results. Hailed by *Romantic Times* as "an exceptional talent with a tremendous gift for involving her readers in the story," Jane Ashford weaves a historical romance between Ariel Harding and the Honorable Alan Gresham, an unlikely alliance that will lead to the discovery of a dark truth and unexpected love in **THE BARGAIN**. National bestselling author Kay Hooper intertwines the lives of two women, strangers who are drawn together by one fatal moment, in **AFTER CAROLINE**. Critically acclaimed author Glenna McReynolds offers us **THE CHALICE AND THE BLADE**, the romantic fantasy of Ceridwen and Dain, struggling to escape the dangers and snares set by friend and foe alike, while discovering that neither can resist the love that promises to bind them forever. And immediately following this page, take a sneak peek at the Bantam women's fiction titles on sale in August.

Don't miss these extraordinary books
by your favorite Bantam authors!

On sale in August:

DARK PARADISE
by Tami Hoag

THE MERMAID
by Betina Krahn

BRIDE OF DANGER
by Katherine O'Neal

DARK PARADISE
by **Tami Hoag**

*Here is nationally bestselling author Tami Hoag's
breathtakingly sensual novel, a story filled with heart-
stopping suspense and shocking passion . . . a story of a
woman drawn to a man as hard and untamable as the
land he loves, and to a town steeped in secrets—where a
killer lurks.*

She could hear the dogs in the distance, baying relentlessly. Pursuing relentlessly, as death pursues life.

Death.

Christ, she was going to die. The thought made
her incredulous. Somehow, she had never really believed this moment would come. The idea had always
loitered in the back of her mind that she would somehow be able to cheat the grim reaper, that she would
be able to deal her way out of the inevitable. She had
always been a gambler. Somehow, she had always
managed to beat the odds. Her heart fluttered and her
throat clenched at the idea that she would not beat
them this time.

The whole notion of her own mortality stunned
her, and she wanted to stop and stare at herself, as if
she were having an out-of-body experience, as if this
person running were someone she knew only in passing. But she couldn't stop. The sounds of the dogs
drove her on. The instinct of self-preservation
spurred her to keep her feet moving.

She lunged up the steady grade of the mountain,
tripping over exposed roots and fallen branches.
Brush grabbed her clothing and clawed her bloodied
face like gnarled, bony fingers. The carpet of decay

on the forest floor gave way in spots as she scrambled, yanking her back precious inches instead of giving her purchase to propel herself forward. Pain seared through her as her elbow cracked against a stone half buried in the soft loam. She picked herself up, cradling the arm against her body, and ran on.

Sobs of frustration and fear caught in her throat and choked her. Tears blurred what sight she had in the moon-silvered night. Her nose was broken and throbbing, forcing her to breathe through her mouth alone, and she tried to swallow the cool night air in great gulps. Her lungs were burning, as if every breath brought in a rush of acid instead of oxygen. The fire spread down her arms and legs, limbs that felt like leaden clubs as she pushed them to perform far beyond their capabilities.

I should have quit smoking. A ludicrous thought. It wasn't cigarettes that was going to kill her. In an isolated corner of her mind, where a strange calm resided, she saw herself stopping and sitting down on a fallen log for a final smoke. It would have been like those nights after aerobics class, when the first thing she had done outside the gym was light up. Nothing like that first smoke after a workout. She laughed, on the verge of hysteria, then sobbed, stumbled on.

The dogs were getting closer. They could smell the blood that ran from the deep cut the knife had made across her face.

There was no one to run to, no one to rescue her. She knew that. Ahead of her, the terrain only turned more rugged, steeper, wilder. There were no people, no roads. There was no hope.

Her heart broke with the certainty of that. No hope. Without hope, there was nothing. All the other systems began shutting down.

She broke from the woods and stumbled into a clearing. She couldn't run another step. Her head swam and pounded. Her legs wobbled beneath her, sending her lurching drunkenly into the open meadow. The commands her brain sent shorted out en route, then stopped firing altogether as her will crumbled.

Strangling on despair, on the taste of her own blood, she sank to her knees in the deep, soft grass and stared up at the huge, brilliant disk of the moon, realizing for the first time in her life how insignificant she was. She would die in this wilderness, with the scent of wildflowers in the air, and the world would go on without a pause. She was nothing, just another victim of another hunt. No one would even miss her. The sense of stark loneliness that thought sent through her numbed her to the bone.

No one would miss her.

No one would mourn her.

Her life meant nothing.

She could hear the crashing in the woods behind her. The sound of hoofbeats. The snorting of a horse. The dogs baying. Her heart pounding, ready to explode.

She never heard the shot.

FROM THE *New York Times* BESTSELLING

BETINA KRAHN

With the wit of *The Last Bachelor*, the charm of *The Perfect Mistress*, and the sparkle of *The Unlikely Angel*, Betina Krahn has penned an enchanting new romance

THE MERMAID

If Celeste Ashton hadn't needed money to save her grandmother's seaside estate, she would never have published her observations on ocean life and the dolphins she has befriended. So when her book makes her an instant celebrity, she is unprepared for the attention . . . especially when it comes from unnervingly handsome Titus Thorne. While Titus suspects there is something fishy about her theories, Celeste is determined to be taken seriously. Soon their fiery ideological clashes create sparks neither expects, and Titus must decide if he will risk his credibility, his career—and his heart—to side with the Lady Mermaid.

"KRAHN HAS A DELIGHTFUL, SMART
TOUCH."
—*Publishers Weekly*

"Miss Ashton, permit me to apologize for what may appear to one outside the scientific community to be rudeness on the part of our members. We are all accustomed to the way the vigorous spirit of inquiry often leads to enthusiastic questioning and debate. The familiarity of long acquaintance and the dogged pursuit of truth sometimes lead us to overstep the bounds of general decorum."

She stared at the tall, dark-haired order bringer, uncertain whether to be irritated or grateful that he had just taken over her lecture.

"I believe I . . . understand."

Glancing about the lecture hall, she was indeed beginning to understand. She had received their invitation to speak as an honor, and had prepared her lecture under the assumption that she was being extended a coveted offer of membership in the societies. But, in fact, she had not been summoned here to *join;* she had been summoned here to *account.* They had issued her an invitation to an inquisition . . . for the grave offense of publishing research without the blessing of the holy orders of science: the royal societies.

"Perhaps if I restated a few of the questions I have heard put forward just now," he said, glancing at the members seated around him, "it would preserve order and make for a more productive exchange."

Despite his handsome smile and extreme mannerliness, her instincts warned that here was no ally.

"You state that most of your observations have been made while you were in the water with the creatures, themselves." As he spoke, he made his way to the end of the row, where the others in the aisle made way for him to approach the front of the stage.

"That is true," she said, noting uneasily the way the others parted for him.

"If I recall correctly, you stated that you sail or row out into the bay waters, rap out a signal on the hull of your boat, and the dolphin comes to greet you. You then slip into the water with the creature—or creatures, if he has brought his family group—hold your breath, and dive under the water to observe them."

"That is precisely what happens. Though I must say, it is a routine perfected by extreme patience and long experience. Years, in fact."

"You expect us to believe you not only call these creatures at will, but that you voluntarily . . . single-handedly . . . climb into frigid water with any number of these monstrous large beasts, and that you swim underwater for hours on end to observe them?" He straightened, glancing at the others as he readied his thrust. "That is a great deal indeed to believe on the word of a young woman who has no scientific training and no formal academic background."

His words struck hard and sank deep. So that was it. She was young and female and intolerably presumptuous to attempt to share her learning and experiences with the world when she hadn't the proper credentials.

"It is true that I have had no formal academic training. But I studied and worked with my grandfather for years; learning the tenants of reason and logic, developing theoretical approaches, observing and recording." She stepped out from behind the podium, facing him, facing them all for the sake of what she knew to be the truth.

"There is much learning, sir, to be had *outside* the hallowed, ivy-covered walls of a university. Experience is a most excellent tutor."

She saw him stiffen as her words found a mark in him. But a moment later, all trace of that fleeting reaction was gone.

"Very well, Miss Ashton, let us proceed and see what your particular brand of science has produced." His words were now tightly clipped, tailored for maximum impact. "You observe underwater, do you not? Just how do you *see* all of these marvels several yards beneath the murky surface?"

"Firstly, ocean water is not 'murky.' Anyone who has spent time at the seaside knows that." She moved to the table and picked up a pair of goggles. "Secondly, I wear these. They are known in sundry forms to divers on various continents."

"Very well, it might work. But several obstacles still remain. Air, for instance. How could you possibly stay under the water long enough to have seen all that you report?"

She looked up at him through fiercely narrowed eyes.

"I hold my breath."

"Indeed? Just how long can you hold your breath, Miss Ashton?"

"Minutes at a time."

"Oh?" His eyebrows rose. "And what proof do you have?"

"Proof? What proof do you need?" she demanded, her hands curling into fists at her sides. "Shall I stick my head in a bucket for you?"

Laughter skittered through their audience, only to die when he shot them a censuring look. "Perhaps we could arrange an impromptu test of your remarkable breathing ability, Miss Ashton. I propose that you hold your breath—right here, right now—and we will time you."

"Don't be ridiculous," she said, feeling crowded by his height and intensity. He stood head and shoulders above her and obviously knew how to use his size to advantage in a confrontation.

"It is anything *but* ridiculous," he declared. "It would be a demonstration of the repeatability of a phenomenon. Repetition of results is one of the key tests of scientific truth, is it not?"

"It would not be a true trial," she insisted, but loathe to mention why. His silence and smug look combined with derogatory comments from the audience to prod it from her. "I am wearing a 'dress improver,'" she said through clenched teeth, "which restricts my breathing."

"Oh. Well." He slid his gaze down to her waist, allowing it to linger there for a second too long. When she glared at him, he smiled. "We can adjust for that by giving you . . . say . . . ten seconds?"

Before she could protest, he called for a mirror to detect stray breath. None could be found on such short notice, so, undaunted, he volunteered to hold a strip of paper beneath her nose to detect any intake of air. The secretary, Sir Hillary, was drafted as a time-keeper and a moment later she was forced to purge her lungs, strain her corset to take in as much air as possible, and then hold it.

Her inquisitor leaned close, holding that fragile strip of paper, watching for the slightest flutter in it. And as she struggled to find the calm center into which she always retreated while diving, she began to feel the heat radiating from him . . . the warmth of his face near her own . . . the energy coming from his broad shoulders. And she saw his eyes, mere inches from hers, beginning to wander over her face. Was he purposefully trying to distract her? Her quickening pulse said that if he was, his tactic was working. To combat it, she searched desperately for someplace to fasten her vision, something to concentrate on. Unfortunately, the closest available thing was *him*.

Green eyes, she realized, with mild surprise. Blue

green, really. The color of sunlight streaming into the sea on a midsummer day. His skin was firm and lightly tanned . . . stretched taut over a broad forehead, high cheekbones, and a prominent, slightly aquiline nose. Her gaze drifted downward to his mouth . . . full, velvety looking, with a prominent dip in the center of his upper lip that made his mouth into an intriguing bow. There were crinkle lines at the corners of his eyes and a beard shadow was forming along the edge of his cheek.

She found herself licking her lip . . . lost in the bold angles and intriguing textures of his very male face . . . straining for control and oblivious to the fact that half of the audience was on its feet and moving toward the stage. She had never observed a man this close for this long—well, besides her grandfather and the brigadier. A man. A handsome man. His hair was a dark brown, not black, she thought desperately. And as her chest began to hurt, she fastened her gaze on his eyes and held on with everything in her. This was for science. This was for her dolphins. This was to teach those sea green eyes a lesson . . .

The ache in her chest gradually crowded everything but him and his eyes from her consciousness. Finally, when she felt the dimming at the edges of her vision, which spelled real danger, she blew out that breath and then gasped wildly. The fresh air was so intoxicating that she staggered.

A wave of astonishment greeted the news that she had held her breath for a full three minutes.

BRIDE OF DANGER
by **Katherine O'Neal**

Winner of the *Romantic Times* Award for Best
Sensual Historical Romance

*Night after night, she graced London's most elegant
soirees, her flame-haired beauty drawing all eyes, her
innocent charm wresting from men the secrets of their
souls. And not one suspected the truth: that she was a
spy, plucked from the squalor of Dublin's filthy streets.
For Mylene, devoted to the cause of freedom, it was a
role she gladly played . . . until the evening she came
face-to-face with the mysterious Lord Whitney. All of the
ton was abuzz with his recent arrival. But only Mylene
knew he was as much of an imposter as she. Gone was
any trace of Johnny, the wild Irish youth she
remembered. In his place was a rogue more devastatingly
handsome than any man had a right to be—and a rebel
coldheartedly determined to do whatever it took to fulfill
his mission. Now he was asking Mylene to betray
everything she'd come to believe in. And even as she
knew she had to stop him, she couldn't resist
surrendering to his searing passion.*

On the boat to England, Mylene had learned her role.
She was to play an English orphan who'd lost her
parents in an Irish uprising and, for want of any rela-
tions, had been shipped home to an English orphan-
age. The story would explain Mylene's knowledge of
Dublin. But more, it was calculated to stir the embers
of her adoptive father Lord Stanley's heart. He was
the staunchest opposition Parliament had to Irish
Home Rule. That Mylene's parents had been killed

by Irish rabble rousers garnered his instant sympathy. He'd taken her in at first glance, and formally adopted her within the year.

In the beginning, Mylene had been flabbergasted by her surroundings. She wasn't certain she could perform such an extended role without giving herself away. The luxurious lifestyle, the formalities and graces, proved matters of extreme discomfort. To be awakened in the warmth of her plush canopied bed with a cup of steaming cocoa embarrassed her as much as being waited on hand and foot. But soon enough, James—the driver who secretly worked for their cause—had passed along her assignment. She was to use her position to discover the scandalous secrets of Lord Stanley's friends and associates. Buoyed by the sense of purpose, she'd thrown herself into her task with relish, becoming accomplished at the subterfuge in no time.

What she hadn't counted on was growing to love Lord Stanley. Ireland, and her old life, began to seem like the dream.

"How fares the Countess?" he asked, thinking she'd gone to visit a friend.

"Well enough, I think, for all that her confinement makes her edgy."

"Well, it's all to a good purpose, as she'll see when the baby comes. But tell me, my dear, did her happy state have its effect? I shouldn't mind a grandchild of my own before too much time."

"The very thing we were discussing when you came in," announced his companion.

Mylene turned and looked at Roger Helmsley. He was a dashing gentleman of thirty years, tall with dark brown hair and a fetching pencil-thin mustache. He wore his evening clothes with negligent ease, secure in his wealth and position. He was Lord Stanley's compatriot in Parliament, the driving force behind the Irish opposition.

"Lord Helmsley has been pressing his suit," explained her father. "He informs me, with the most dejected of countenances, that he's asked for your hand on three separate occasions. Yet he says you stall him with pretty smiles."

"She's a coy one, my lord," said Roger, coming to take both her hands in his. "I daresay some of your own impeccable diplomacy has rubbed off on your daughter."

"Is this a conspiracy?" she laughed. "Is a girl not to be allowed her say?"

"If you'd say anything at all, I might bear up. But this blasted silence on the subject . . . Come, my sweet. What must an old bachelor like myself do to entice the heart of such a fair maiden?"

Roger was looking at her with a glow of appreciation that to this day made her flush with wonder. At twenty-two, Mylene had blossomed under the Earl's care. The rich food from his table had transformed the scrawny street urchin into a woman with enticing curves. Her breasts were full, her hips ripe and rounded, her legs nicely lean and defined from hours in the saddle and long walks through Hyde Park. Her skin, once so sallow, glowed with rosy health. Even her riotous curls glistened with rich abundance. Her pouty mouth was legendary among the swells of Marlboro House. Her clothes were fashioned by the best dressmakers in London, giving her a regal, polished air—if one didn't look too closely at the impish scattering of freckles across her nose. But when she looked in the mirror, she always gave a start of surprise. She thought of herself still as the ill-nourished orphan without so much as a last name.

It was partly this quest for a family of her own that had her considering Roger's proposal. He was an affable and decent man who, on their outings, had displayed a free-wheeling sense of the absurd that had brought an element of fun to her sadly serious life. His wealth, good looks, and charm were the talk of mothers with marriageable daughters. And if his politics appalled her, she'd learned long ago from Lord Stanley that a man could hold differing, even dangerous political views, and still be the kindest of men. Admittedly, the challenge intrigued her. As his wife, she could perhaps influence him to take a more liberal stance.

"You see how she avoids me," Roger complained in a melodramatic tone.

There was a knock on the door before the panels were slid open by Jensen, the all-too-proper majordomo who'd been in the service of Lord Stanley's grandfather. "Excuse the intrusion, my lord, but a gentleman caller awaits your pleasure without."

"A caller?" asked Lord Stanley. "At this hour?"

"His card, my lord."

Lord Stanley took the card. "Good gracious. Lord Whitney. Send him in, Jensen, by all means."

When Jensen left with a stiff bow, Roger asked, "A jest perhaps? A visit from the grave?"

"No, no, my good man. Not old Lord Whitney. It's his son. I'd heard on his father's death that he was on his way. Been in India with his mother since he was a lad. As you know, the climate agreed with her, and she refused to return when her husband's service was at an end. Kept the boy with her. We haven't seen the scamp since he was but a babe."

"Well, well, this *is* news! It's our duty, then, to set

him straight right from the start. Curry his favor, so to speak. We shouldn't want the influence he's inherited to go the wrong way."

"He's his father's son. He'll see our way of things, I'll warrant."

Mylene knew what this meant. Old Lord Whitney, while ill and with one foot in the grave, had nevertheless roused himself to Parliament in his wheelchair to lambaste, in his raspy voice, the MPs who favored Ireland's pleas. Lord Stanley, she knew, was counting on the son to take up the cause. It meant another evening of feeling her hackles rise as the gentlemen discussed new ways to squelch the Irish rebellion.

She kept her lashes lowered, cautioning herself to silence, as the gentleman stepped into the room and the doors were closed behind him.

Lord Stanley greeted him. "Lord Whitney, what a pleasant surprise. I'd planned to call on you myself, as soon as I'd heard you'd arrived. May I express my condolences for your father's passing. He was a distinguished gentleman, and a true friend. I assure you, he shall be missed by all."

Mylene felt the gentleman give a gracious bow.

"Allow me to present my good friend, Lord Helmsley. You'll be seeing a great deal of each other, I don't doubt."

The men shook hands.

"And this, sir, is my daughter, Mylene. Lord Whitney, from India."

Mylene set her face in courteous lines. But when she glanced up, the smile of welcome froze on her face.

It was Johnny!

On sale in September:

AFTER CAROLINE
by Kay Hooper

WHEN YOU WISH . . .
by Jane Feather, Patricia Coughlin, Sharon & Tom Curtis, Elizabeth Elliot, Patricia Potter, and Suzanne Robinson

THE BARGAIN
by Jane Ashford

THE CHALICE AND THE BLADE
by Glenna McReynolds

DON'T MISS THESE FABULOUS
BANTAM WOMEN'S FICTION TITLES

On Sale in September

AFTER CAROLINE by Kay Hooper

A sensuous novel about the bewildering connection between two strangers who look enough alike to be twins. When one of them mysteriously dies, the survivor searches for the truth—was Caroline's death an accident, or was she the target of a killer willing to kill again?

___57184-2 $5.99/$7.99

WHEN YOU WISH...
by Jane Feather, Patricia Coughlin, Sharon & Tom Curtis, Elizabeth Elliott, Patricia Potter, and Suzanne Robinson

National bestseller Jane Feather leads a talent-packed line-up in this enchanting collection of six original—and utterly romantic—short stories. A mysterious bottle containing one wish falls into the hands of each of the heroines...with magical results. ___57643-7 $5.99/$7.99

THE BARGAIN
by Jane Ashford, author of THE MARRIAGE WAGER

When a maddeningly forthright beauty and an arrogant, yet undeniably attractive scientist team up to rid London of a mysterious ghost, neither plans on the most confounding of all scientific occurrences: the breathless chemistry of desire. ___57578-3 $5.99/$7.99

THE CHALICE AND THE BLADE
by Glenna McReynolds

In a novel of dark magic, stirring drama, and fierce passion, the daughter of a Druid priestess and a feared sorcerer unlock the mystery of an ancient legacy. ___10384-9 $16.00/$22.95

Ask for these books at your local bookstore or use this page to order.

Please send me the books I have checked above. I am enclosing $____ (add $2.50 to cover postage and handling). Send check or money order, no cash or C.O.D.'s, please.

Name _____

Address _____

City/State/Zip _____

Send order to: Bantam Books, Dept. FN158, 2451 S. Wolf Rd., Des Plaines, IL 60018
Allow four to six weeks for delivery.
Prices and availability subject to change without notice. FN 158 9/97